The New Boy Who Hears Buzzing

DETECTIVE DOVE

ZUNI BLUE

AMARIA & SARIEL

LONDON

THE NEW BOY WHO HEARS BUZZING

Text Copyright © 2013 Zahra Brown (pseudonym: 'Zuni Blue')

Cover Design Copyright © 2019 Zahra Brown

Cover Illustration by Fenny Fu

For more information, please contact:

Zuni Blue at www.zuniblue.com

Print ISBN: 978-1097691029

First Edition August 2013

This Edition May 2019

100 Free Gifts For You

There are 100 FREE printables waiting for you!

Certificates, bookmarks, wallpapers and more! You can choose your favourite colour: red, yellow, pink, green, orange, purple or blue.

You don't need money or an email address. Check out www.zuniblue.com to print your free gifts today.

CONTENTS

Case File No.3

In London, England, you'll find Detective Inspector Mya Dove. With four years' experience on the police force, this eight-year-old is on her way to being the best police officer ever.

Yes. The best. Her mum said so.

To inspire other kids, she's sharing case files. Case File No. 3: The New Boy Who Hears Buzzing.

Chapter 1

On Monday afternoon, Mrs Cherry looked very excited. I mean more excited than usual. Her furry, red eyebrows were twitching like crazy. This always happened before she gave us a scrapbook project…

I couldn't wait to start!

I'd already picked my scrapbook topic: it was all about bugs! No, not bugs like insects, I mean bugs like police bugs.

A police bug is a tiny, secret microphone officers use to record bad guys. When no one else is around, bad guys say very naughty things. They think no one can hear them, but they're wrong.

I'd used police bugging ever since Dad bought me a voice recorder. I left it in the kitchen and caught my big brother Will saying, "I'm gonna eat Mya's chocolate." I played the recording to my parents. They made Will say sorry and buy me TWO new chocolates.

If I hadn't bugged the kitchen, I would never have known who took my chocolate. That's why I wanted to do my scrapbook on police bugs. Bugs were very helpful and everyone should know about them!

I crossed my fingers and hoped Mrs Cherry was giving us another scrapbook project. It was *so* much fun! I loved finding pictures and sticking them down. Next, I'd write something under each picture to explain it. To finish off, I always decorated the scrapbook's cover with photos.

Please let us do scrapbooks, I thought. Please, please, please…

"Can anyone guess what exciting news I have today?" Mrs Cherry asked.

"Are we giving speeches again?" Angel asked. Angel was the meanest girl in school. All her friends were mean too. "I love giving speeches!"

"No, try again."

Angel smiled at Mrs Cherry, but her blue eyes looked really mad. She hated not getting what she wanted.

My best friend Libby nudged me. She whispered her question for me to ask.

Libby had social anxiety, so speaking to people made her really, really nervous. I'd agreed to ask questions for her.

I put my hand up before speaking.

"Miss, Libby has a question," I said.

"I'd love to hear it!"

"Libby was wondering if we're doing group work again?"

"Libby is right, we are. A joint scrapbook."

Everyone gasped. We hadn't done a joint scrapbook before.

"So, class, what will the scrapbook topic be about?"

Everyone looked shocked. Usually we did our scrapbook on whatever we liked. This time Mrs Cherry was giving us a topic.

But that means I can't do my scrapbook on police bugs, I thought sadly. Oh man…

"Class, the scrapbook topic has been chosen by me! You'll create an amazing scrapbook about…Henry the Eighth! He was King of England hundreds of years ago. Does anyone know how many wives he had?"

Angel put her hand up. Other people did too, but she gave them a mean look. They slowly put their hands down.

"Miss, *I* know the answer," Angel said, flicking her blonde curls. "King Henry had six wives."

"Can anyone name them all?" Mrs Cherry asked.

"I think I can," my friend Jimmy said. "Um, Catherine—"

"Me too," Angel snapped. "Catherine, Anne, Jane, Anne, Catherine, and...Catherine."

I couldn't imagine six mums telling me off! One was bad enough...

"Thank you, Jimmy. Angel, try not to interrupt again."

"Sorry Jimmy," Angel said. She gave him an angry look. "He was taking so long to answer. I just wanted to help him."

Jimmy shrugged it off before picking at a big, red spot on his white face.

"Anyway, the class will be split into six groups. Each group will focus on one of Henry's wives…"

While Mrs Cherry talked about our scrapbook project, Jimmy gave me a nudge. He tossed a folded paper into my hand. I waited before reading it, just in case someone was watching.

I slowly unfolded the paper and placed it on my desk. I kept my eyes on Mrs Cherry.

"Class, this is just the beginning of our royal scrapbook projects. There are so many other royal families around the world!"

When Mrs Cherry looked away, I glanced at the secret note from Jimmy. It said:

Don't speak!
They can hear us!

I froze.

Who was listening? Where were they? Were they listening to the whole class or just the officers in the Children's Police Force?

I leaned over to ask Jimmy for more info, but he put his finger to his lips. He looked scared. Now I was scared too.

"Class, who would like to be in Angel's group?"

Only Angel's friends put their hands up. Mrs Cherry wrote their names on the whiteboard.

"Okay, I'm assuming that Ahmarri, Emma, Mya, Jimmy and Libby will be working together…" Mrs Cherry looked at Jimmy, a puzzled look on her face. "What's the matter?"

Everyone looked at Jimmy. He'd been fine a minute ago. I thought maybe he was worried about the note.

But it wasn't the note. It was his eye.

Jimmy kept rubbing it until it was bright pink and teary.

"Jimmy, what's wrong with your eye?" Mrs Cherry asked.

Jimmy kept rubbing until a tear trickled down his cheek.

"Jimmy, would you like to come up here, please?"

"Something's in my eye," Jimmy said. "Mya said she saw it, right?"

I nodded, not knowing what was going on. But I trusted him. He'd helped me out before. It was time for me to help him.

"Let me see your eye, dear."

"Mya has an eye rinse. Can I use it?"

"Let me help—"

"The eye rinse is in my bag," I said quickly. "We can't use it here. It'll be a distraction."

"James, Mya, let me—"

"Thank you, Mya," Jimmy said. "Let's go out to the corridor!"

"Oh, I give up!" Mrs Cherry threw her hands up. "Just hurry back, please."

Mrs Cherry motioned to the door. We hurried out before she changed her mind.

In the corridor, Jimmy put his hand over my mouth and pulled me into the boys' toilets. I covered my eyes just in case.

"Jim—"

"Quiet," he hissed. "Gimme a sec."

He went to the sinks and turned on each cold tap at full blast. I could barely hear him over the noisy water running down the plughole.

"Okay, they can't hear us anymore," he said. "We can chat now."

"What's going on?" I asked.

I was feeling even more nervous now. Jimmy had never looked this scared before.

Things had to be really bad.

"They're listening," he said. "They're *always* listening."

"Who?"

"You won't believe me when I tell you this but..."

Jimmy bit his lip and looked away.

"Jimmy, just say it," I said. "Hurry up! Mrs Cherry will wonder what's taking us so long."

"Mya, I think we've been bugged by the *real* police..."

Chapter 2

I burst out laughing. I couldn't believe that Jimmy thought the adult police force would bug our school. It didn't make any sense.

"Jimmy, why would they bug us?"

"To keep an eye on us, I guess." He scratched his spotty cheek. "I know it sounds crazy, but who else bugs people? Only the police, right?"

I couldn't think of anyone else who bugged people, but I didn't believe the adult police would bug us. That wasn't a nice thing to do!

"Who's been bugged?" I asked.

"One of the new boys. His name is Ricky Miles. He's only four."

That made me angry. Four years old? He was just a kid! Why would the police bug a new boy? It was hard enough being the new kid.

The police wouldn't bug a new kid, but bad guys would. They didn't care if doing something was mean or not. They just did whatever they wanted.

"How do you know he's been bugged?" I asked.

"He keeps hearing a buzzing noise. No one else can hear it."

A buzzing noise only one person could hear. I'd never heard of something like that before.

"Where's the bug?" I asked.

"I think it's a tiny microphone in his ears

somewhere. We checked his hair for bugs, but only found some lice and old chewing gum."

Yuck!

Not finding a police bug in Ricky's hair made perfect sense. The adult police didn't bug hair. They bugged houses and cars. When the case was closed, they took all the bugs out.

Bad guys would probably bug someone's ears. If the bug got stuck in some earwax, it'd never come out. Then the bad guys could bug the person forever and ever.

"We have to help him," Jimmy said. "Just talking about his buzzing ears makes him cry."

I imagined poor little Ricky crying. It made me feel so sad. How could someone bug a nursery kid? It was *so* mean!

"Mya, things are really hard for him right

now. He's got a test next week at nursery. He'll have to write his full name, draw five different shapes and count all the way to fifty!"

To fifty? That was a tough one at his age.

"Jimmy, it sounds like he really is being bugged." I leaned in closer and so did he. Our noses were touching. "If we don't stop that bug, WE might be bugged next!"

Jimmy's eyes widened. We both knew I was right.

"Ricky's bug doesn't sound like a normal police bug to me," I said. "Normal police bugs aren't put in people's hair or ears. And the police don't ever bug kids!"

"So these must be bad guys' bugs?"

"Exactly!"

Our school was being bugged by bad guys. The bad guys were trying to find out our secrets. They were too scared to bug police officers like me or Jimmy, so they went after a new boy like Ricky instead.

If Jimmy and I didn't do something soon, we'd *all* have bugs in our ears. We couldn't let that happen. We worked for the Children's Police Force. It was our job to keep everyone safe.

If the bad guys hid bugs all over our school, they could listen to us talking. That meant they'd know all our plans, every case we solved, and every bad guy we kept an eye on. The bad guys would know all our police secrets and stop us solving cases!

"It's too late to start the case today," I said. "Tell Ricky to meet us at the nursery gate tomorrow morning at breaktime. Tell him to come alone. We can't trust anyone right now."

"…Can you trust me?"

"Of course! Get there early. Oh, and bring

a small metal detector."

"Why?" he asked.

"You'll see..."

Chapter 3

The nursery kids were much younger than us. They were only three or four years old. I was eight, almost nine. They had their own playground because we were bigger than them.

The nursery playground was AMAZING. They had a really slippery slide, huge sandpit, paddling pool, the coolest climbing frame and loads of toys.

All the older kids were jealous. We got lots of work. Nursery kids got lots of toys. We had to work for the whole day. They only had half-days, and less than that if they felt homesick.

Sometimes older kids went to the nursery gate just to see the cool stuff younger kids had. We weren't allowed past the gate without permission from a teacher. That's why Jimmy and I waited at the gate for Ricky to come over.

Ricky showed up with tears in his small, green eyes. I reached over the gate and gave him a tissue.

"Is the noise *that* bad today?" Jimmy asked.

Ricky nodded.

"I've brought some help," Jimmy said. "This is Detective—"

"Quiet," I hissed. "Don't say my whole name! *They* might be listening."

We all checked over our shoulders. I couldn't see anyone watching us, but they could've been hiding in the bushes or behind the big tree in the playground.

"We'll check you for bugs before we talk," I said. "Officer, give me the metal detector, please."

Jimmy handed the small metal detector over. I turned it on and tested it out on my earrings. Even though my earrings were tiny studs, the metal detector bleeped loudly when it was next to them.

"Ricky, stand very still." I held the metal detector next to his head. "This should only take a minute."

Ricky nodded, shaking from fear.

"Jimmy, I mean *officer* please look out for any teachers!"

Jimmy turned away, watching over the playground. When he said it was safe, I unlocked the nursery gate and opened it a little. Just wide enough to get my arm through.

Ricky moved closer to me. Slowly, I moved the metal detector all over his body.

First, I checked Ricky's head. The metal detector didn't make any noise when I ran it over his shiny, red hair. The bug definitely wasn't there. I did find lice though, and told Ricky he needed to buy some special lice shampoo.

"There's no bug in your hair," I said. "Open your mouth, please."

I held the metal detector over his mouth.

Bleep! Bleep! Bleep! The detector's red light turned bright green. Ricky's chubby face turned as white as the clouds.

"The bad guys must've put the bug in his mouth," I cried. "Let me see!"

Jimmy held Ricky's mouth open while I looked around inside. I used my pen that had a torch on the end.

His teeth looked normal except for a filling. I couldn't see a tiny microphone bug in there.

"The filling set off the detector," I said. "It wasn't a bug."

Jimmy and Ricky sighed with relief.

"We're not done yet," I said quickly. "Let's try your arms."

The metal detector didn't make any noise when I checked his arms. No noise when I moved down his stomach and back either. That was good. It meant he hadn't eaten the bug by accident.

"So far it's good news," I said. "Let's try your legs and feet."

Once again, the metal detector didn't find anything. There was nothing in his scruffy shorts, white socks or new trainers.

It was good news that the bug wasn't on him…but if the bug wasn't on him, where was it?

"Are you sure you can hear a bug?" I asked.

"It's buzzing in my ears all the time." Ricky stuck a finger in each ear and sighed sadly. "The noise is still there! It's louder now."

I closed the nursery gate and gave the metal detector back to Jimmy.

"Ricky, turn your head and hold still."

I shone the torch in his ear and took a closer look. What I saw was gross! There was golden-coloured earwax inside. When I checked his other ear, it was just as bad in there.

"Ricky, your ears have lots of wax in them. You need a good cleaning!"

"Could that make my ears buzz?"

"Maybe, I don't know. You'll have to clean your ears to find out."

"If it's not wax, could it be..." Ricky

checked over his shoulders before speaking again. "Aliens! Could the buzzing be from aliens? Maybe some cool ones from Mars."

Jimmy and I looked at each other. He looked as confused as I was.

"Ricky," I said, "we think you were bugged by people, not aliens. They put a very tiny microphone on you somewhere we can't find it. The microphone is buzzing because some things buzz or hum when they're turned on."

"I still think it could be aliens," Ricky said, looking up at the sky. "I think I got taken by aliens last year. They took me into their flying spaceship. We had sparkly milkshakes and played video games all day. Then I woke up."

"Okay…" I said. "Well, I don't know about all that."

"My grandad saw a TV show about aliens

talking to people," Ricky said, still staring at the sky. "Do you think aliens are talking to me? Maybe they want to take me to Mars?"

If aliens took anyone, they'd probably take mean girls like Angel because no one wanted them around.

"Maybe that's why you can't find the microphone," Ricky said, looking at me. "Because alien microphones are harder to find! The metal detector doesn't work for them, maybe?"

"Unless..." Jimmy bit his lip, his face sweaty. He looked around the playground and edged closer to the nursery gate. I moved closer too.

"Go on," I whispered.

"If they didn't bug Ricky, maybe they bugged the school!"

"Ricky, do you hear the buzzing at home or only at school?"

"Definitely at school," he said. "The buzzing gets quieter in the car on the way home. At home, my big brothers play loud video games and really loud music. I don't hear any buzzing in my house."

Jimmy had to be right. The bug wasn't on Ricky, it was in the playground or school building. That's why the buzzing noise was quieter when Ricky left school.

The bug could even be on students, teachers, the caretaker, the dinner ladies, the school nurse, the receptionist, or even Mr Badal, the meanest headteacher in the world.

The bug could even be on me!

"Put your hands up," I told Jimmy. I checked him with the metal detector. It went off when I reached his pocket.

"Open up," I said.

Jimmy opened his pockets. Inside were handcuffs, two pens and his police badge.

The police badge was made of metal, so it set the detector's alarm off.

"Your turn," Jimmy said, taking the detector from me.

He checked me over from head to toe. Again, only my earrings made the detector's alarm go off.

When we'd finished checking each other, we all sighed with relief. The bug wasn't on us. It was hidden somewhere else at school.

"We'll check the whole school," I said. "Every bush, every tree, every bin, every drawer, every person, everything! I'll use the metal detector on everything until I find that microphone. Then we'll know who bugged our school."

Jimmy didn't look so sure.

"Mya, it'll be easy to check bins and bushes, but how do we check people? We can't go around checking everybody with the metal detector."

He was right. Nice people like my friend Libby wouldn't mind being checked. Mean people like Angel, the most horrible girl in the world, wouldn't let us check them.

There was also the chance that mean people like Angel were working with the bad guys. That meant we had to keep all the metal detector checks a secret.

"How can we check everyone without them knowing?" I asked. "Wait, I have an idea!"

On Wednesday morning, we were having a school assembly. Sometimes we all got together to sing songs. Some lucky people got to play instruments.

Other assemblies were more boring, like listening to teachers tell us off about something.

"The whole school will be there," I

whispered. "It'll be the best time to check everyone."

The only people who wouldn't be there were the dinner ladies, caretaker and headteacher. We could always check them for bugs later.

My plan was simple: before assembly started, check every student with the metal detector. We could check teachers too.

Someone could be listening through the bugs, so I whispered my plan to Jimmy and Ricky.

"Who's gonna do the checks?" Jimmy asked. "Me, you or Ricky?"

"None of us."

"What?" they both cried.

"Someone else will check everyone for us," I said. "I know just who to ask..."

We needed help from someone who teachers and students both liked. If this person checked people with a metal detector, nobody would complain about it.

"Jimmy, there's someone important we need to see. We'll meet him at lunchtime."

My plan was simple. First, we'd speak to my friend and he'd help us check everyone for bugs. Next, we'd find the tiny bug and turn it off. Ricky's ears would stop buzzing.

The Children's Police Force would use the bug to find the bad guys and lock them away in detention. Then the case would be closed.

I'd be rewarded with the tastiest fruit in the whole world: some juicy, green grapes. After that, everything would go back to normal.

Well, that's what I thought would happen, but I was wrong.

Very, very wrong...

Chapter 4

At lunchtime, Jimmy and I waited by the door. We quickly ate our sandwiches and had our drinks. Then we waited patiently for my friend to come.

"Is he really one of us?" Jimmy asked quietly. "Your friend?"

"He's the top police officer at school," I replied. "Our bosses have to do as he says."

Jimmy took out his police badge and shined it on his sleeve. His hands were shaking the whole time.

Meanwhile, I wrote an important note on

some paper. To keep it a secret, I folded it and wrote TO JAMAR on top. Hopefully no one else would read it.

The door flew open and Year Six walked in. Everyone got out of their way. The older kids were not only bigger than us but smarter too. They always got the most homework and the toughest exams.

"Year Six is here," Jimmy said. "Which one's your friend?"

"The one at the back."

There was a tall, biracial boy walking behind the others. His friends ruffled his curly, dark brown hair, so he playfully pushed them off. Then he tidied his creased jumper and fixed his wonky Prefect badge.

When the biracial boy and his friends were close by, I threw the folded paper on the floor. It landed by the boy's feet.

"To Jamar," he said. "Interesting…"

Quickly, he scooped up the paper and slipped it into his pocket. He did it so fast no one else seemed to notice.

"That's him, right?" Jimmy whispered.

"Yes, that's my friend Jamar."

Jamar was in Year Six. As the Chief Superintendent, he was the top officer at our school's Children's Police Force. We worked together on my last big case, but we hadn't spoken much since.

"If you ever need anything, just ask," Jamar once told me. "I'll help you. I promise."

Today I needed his help. If anyone could stop the bad guys bugging our school, it was Jamar. He'd help get rid of every single secret microphone. Then the bad guys couldn't spy on us anymore.

When lunchtime was over, everyone went out to play. Jimmy and I waited in the playground, keeping an eye out for Jamar.

Year Six came outside and ran off to play. Only Jamar and his friends were left behind.

Suddenly Jamar spun to face Jimmy and me. He pointed at the blue Prefect badge on his jumper and marched over to us.

"No standing around," Jamar yelled at me. "Go and play!"

I didn't know what to say. I looked at Jimmy, who just shrugged and backed away.

"Jamar, it's me," I said quietly. "Mya!"

"I know," he whispered, "but I can't be seen talking to some Year Four kids. My friends will laugh at me again."

Jamar winked at me. I nodded back.

"Sorry, Prefect," I said, pulling a sad face.

"Go to the bench and sit down," Jamar ordered. "I need to tell you kids off for five minutes!"

Jamar's friends shrugged and walked

away. Now Jimmy, Jamar and I were alone. We went to the bench and sat down.

"Hi, Mya," Jamar said. "Nice to see you again."

"You too!"

"James, nice to meet you," Jamar said to Jimmy. "We never introduced ourselves last time, did we?"

Jimmy shook his head, his mouth gaping open. He knew so many people at school, but he'd never met someone so important before. Jamar was not only the best Prefect at school, but also the best police officer and the smartest student. He was top of everything!

"How can I help you guys?" Jamar asked.

I explained all about the bugs. Some bad guys had put a microphone in school and Ricky could hear it buzzing. I also told him we'd checked Ricky's ears. Besides some yucky earwax, there was nothing else there.

"You're right," Jamar said.

"About what?" I asked.

"You said the adult police don't bug kids. It's got to be criminals doing it."

"Criminals are bad guys, right?" I asked. Jamar nodded, his face turning dark red.

"What's wrong?" I asked.

"I'm the Chief Superintendent," Jamar said. "I'm supposed to look after you guys. Now our school's been bugged! How could I let this happen?"

"You've got lots of Year Six work to do," I said. "The bad guys knew you'd be too busy to notice the bugs. That's not your fault."

"Thanks, Mya. It just makes me so mad that bad guys are spying on us." Jamar clenched his fists. "They could be listening right now…"

He lowered his voice and edged closer to us. Not too close, though. We didn't want his friends to know we got along with each other.

"How can I help?" Jamar asked.

"In assembly tomorrow, use a metal detector to check everyone on the way in. They'll let you do it because you're a Prefect. Everyone likes Prefects."

"But not everyone will be there tomorrow," Jamar said. "Mr Badal, the dinner ladies, nurses and Mr Murphy might skip assembly."

Mr Murphy was the caretaker. We barely saw him or the nurses.

"When can we check them, then?" I asked.

"I'll check them all right now," Jamar said. "Leave it to me, okay?"

I knew we could count on him. He never let our school down. That's why he was the best police officer in the Children's Police Force.

But we couldn't let him do *all* the work…

"What can we do to help?" I asked.

"You and James need to check the playground. Every bush, every bench, behind the tree, the water fountain. Remember to check the nursery. The bug could be in there somewhere."

It was a lot of work to do. How could we check every bush, all the flowers, the toybox, footballs, basketballs, skipping ropes, hula hoops, water fountain, trampoline, climbing frame…How could we check *everything* before the bell rang?

"I'll check inside the main school building," Jamar said. "You should look around outside ASAP!"

Jamar's friends were coming back. They gave me a mean look, and gave an even meaner look to Jimmy.

"See you guys later," Jamar whispered.

"Thanks for helping!" I said.

"No problem."

He stood up and glared at us.

"Don't make me tell you again," he shouted. "Go off and play!"

Jimmy and I pretended to look sad.

"What about the metal detector?" I whispered. "We've only got one. We can't all use it at the same time."

"I have five hidden at school," he said. "A police officer should always be prepared. You never know what you might need. Remember that."

Jamar waved at his friends before hurrying into school.

"Bye, Jamar," Jimmy said quietly. "Wow…the Chief Superintendent…Wow."

We didn't have time to sit around. Jamar was checking inside the main school building. Jimmy and I had to check the playground. I didn't think there was enough time, but we had to try!

"Jimmy, get up," I said. "We have twenty-five minutes to check the whole playground and everything in it."

Jimmy's eyes moved around the playground and back to me. He shook his head sadly.

"We have to try!" I said.

"What if we run out of time?"

"Jamar is inside searching by himself." I grabbed Jimmy's hand and pulled him up. "At least we have each other."

Jimmy started laughing his head off.

"Mya, that's so cheesy!" He giggled. "At least we have each other?"

I pulled my hand away and crossed my arms in a huff. My face was burning because I was so angry. If I wasn't a black person, my face would've turned red.

"Sorry!" he said, smiling at me. "I was just

teasing you, that's all! Of course we'll find that bug in time!"

I wasn't in the mood for his silly games. Besides, we didn't have time to waste. We had to find the secret microphone ASAP!

When we started looking for the bug, I knew we'd find it. We HAD to or the Children's Police Force would be in serious trouble.

We'll find it, I thought to myself.

I was right. We *would* find the bug, and it would be the biggest, strangest-looking bug ever...

Chapter 5

Jimmy and I set off to look around the playground. We only had twenty-five minutes to find the hidden bug. Once we found it, we'd turn it off. Then Ricky wouldn't hear the buzzing noise anymore.

"Are you ready to start?" I asked.

"Let's do this!" Jimmy said.

First, we used the metal detector to check every bench. The detector did bleep a lot, but only because the benches had metal legs and arms.

Second, we used the metal detector on the

bushes. We crawled into every bush and held the detector over each flower, thorn and leaf. We even stuck the detector into the soil, just in case the bug was buried. The detector didn't bleep and the red light never turned green.

Next, we checked the small toybox by the door. The metal detector bleeped over and over again. It wasn't a bug setting off the alarm. It was metal toys like cars and trains.

It didn't take long to search the tree or wooden fences around the playground. There was no bug, and nothing left to check.

"What now?" Jimmy asked, wiping his sweaty brow. "We've looked everywhere."

"Not everywhere," I said. "We haven't checked the nursery yet."

"But we can't go inside. Not without permission from a teacher."

He was right. Nursery kids were small.

Nobody wanted them to get hurt. They might be if they played with bigger kids like us. That's why they had their own play area and toys. The nursery fence kept our playground separate from theirs.

We needed to check the nursery, but no teacher would give us permission without a very good reason. Helping Ricky was a good reason, but we couldn't tell them the truth because the bug might be listening. Then the bad guys would hear about our investigation and stop us from solving the case.

"I've got an idea," Jimmy cried. "Ricky said he wants to be a police officer someday. He could start his police training with this case!"

"Great idea!" I said. "Ricky could check the nursery for bugs."

"If he does well, he could get a badge soon." Jimmy rubbed his chin in deep thought. "I got my badge when I was three. He's four."

That made me a bit jealous. I got my first badge when I was four. My mum saw it at the pound shop and bought it for me.

Jimmy and I went over to the nursery gate. It was bolted shut like always.

Standing near the gate was Ricky. He rushed over and burst into tears. I gave him a tissue, so he wiped his puffy, pink eyes.

"The noise is really bad now," Ricky said. "Buzzzzzz. Buzzzzzz. Buzzzzz. All the time. I don't want to hear it anymore!"

"It'll be okay," I told him. "We're going to find the bug and catch the bad guys. They won't get away with this, I promise!"

"But first, Ricky, we've got to check the nursery playground." Jimmy reached over the gate and handed Ricky the metal detector. "If you want to join the Children's

Police Force, now's the time to start!"

Ricky grabbed the metal detector and jumped up and down. He turned the detector on and started checking the fence. The detector only bleeped when it touched the gate's lock and screws.

"Check the playhouse," I told him.

Ricky went into the playhouse and closed the door behind him. It was hard to spot him through the tiny playhouse windows. I just managed to catch him going upstairs and back down again.

A moment later, Ricky was back outside with us. He shook his head sadly.

"Now try the toybox," I said.

Ricky went to the massive toybox and checked every toy. Without being asked, he even went around the playground and checked the toys other kids were playing with.

On his way back to us, Ricky stopped by the sandpit. His eyes went to me. I nodded. He looked at Jimmy, who gave a thumbs up.

Ricky jumped into the sandpit and started digging around. He'd dig a hole, stick the metal detector inside and waited a second before moving somewhere else.

Soon the sandpit looked like a dog had been burying bones in it. There were holes all over the place. Behind Ricky were piles of sand and loads of soft toys he'd found.

"If he doesn't find it in there," Jimmy said, "he'll have to check inside the nursery. What if his teacher catches him with the metal detector? Will it be taken away?"

I hoped not. We could borrow one of Jamar's metal detectors, but I didn't want to. I wanted to show Jamar how good we were at solving cases. He could tell the Children's Police Force how well we'd done. Then maybe my mean, secret boss would be nicer to me and give me some juicy, green grapes! Probably not…but I had to try, right?

Bleeeeeeeeeeeeeeep!

Ricky turned to face us, his face turning white as a clean bed sheet.

"He found something," I said.

"Dig it up," Jimmy cried. "Dig it up!"

Ricky dropped the metal detector and started digging with both hands. Sand flew over his head and out of the sandpit. Deeper and deeper down he got until there was a massive hole. Then he stopped digging and just stared.

"What is it?" I cried. "Ricky, say something!"

Ricky lay down in the sandpit and rested his ear on something down below. I stood on tiptoes but I still couldn't see what he was looking at.

"Ricky, say something!" Jimmy said. "What's down there?"

Ricky sat up and turned towards us, a frown on his face.

"The noise is louder down there," he said. "I think I found the bug…"

Chapter 6

Ricky brought the bug over to us. It didn't look like any police bug I'd seen on TV shows.

Police bugs were tiny microphones. They were very hard to spot, so they could be hidden anywhere. That's why bad guys didn't know they were there.

But the bug Ricky found wasn't tiny at all...

This bug was a rusty tin can tied to another one with string. I placed one can to my ear but couldn't hear anything. Jimmy tried listening through the other can, shaking his head afterwards.

"I can't hear anything," Jimmy said.

I jumped from fright. I'd heard him! I'd heard his voice through the can next to my ear.

"Move away a bit," I said. "This time, whisper to me."

We moved apart and Jimmy whispered into the can. I could hear him when the can was next to my ear.

"Are they using this to bug us?" Jimmy said into the can.

"I think so," I said back. "The bad guys hide somewhere and listen to everything through the can. They bury the string so no one sees it. When someone talks near to one can, the bad guys hear everything in the other one."

"I think the sound goes down the string

and out the other can," Jimmy said. "I don't know how it works, but it does."

I was glad that we'd found the bug, but how could we turn it off? The cans didn't have an off button to press.

"How do we turn off the bug?" I asked Jimmy.

"I've got an idea," he said. "Ricky, we need your help again."

Jimmy handed the bug back to Ricky. Ricky held it as far away from his body as he possibly could.

"Ricky," Jimmy said, "put the bug in the water table but BE VERY CAREFUL! Water and electrics are dangerous together."

Trembling, Ricky slowly walked towards the water table. He stopped close by and took a deep breath. Jimmy and I took a deep breath too.

"Go on, Ricky!" I cried. "You can do it!"

"When the electrics go in the water, the bug will stop working," Jimmy said.

"But what about the water?" I asked. "Will it be safe to play in afterwards?"

"Oh...hadn't thought of that." Jimmy's eyes widened. "No one can play in water if there's something electrical in it. They'll get hurt really bad."

Stopping Ricky's ears from buzzing was very important, but I couldn't let anyone get hurt. Especially not the little nursery kids.

"Don't do it," I cried. "Give us the bug back, please."

Ricky sighed happily as he handed it back.

"What if we cut the string?" I asked. "You said the sound is going down the string. If we cut the string then the sound can't go down it anymore."

"But we can't cut it," Jimmy said. "My dad cut a wire in our house and blew a fuse.

All the lights went out and my mum told him off."

"So if we cut the string and there's electrics in it, we might get hurt?"

He nodded.

"So what do we do then?"

"Let's just get rid of it," he said. "I don't think we can recycle string, so let's just put the bug in the giant bin behind the kitchen."

It was a good idea. The giant food bins were packed with leftovers. The bug would be buried under the old, mouldy food. Then the bad guys couldn't listen to us anymore.

Even better, the food might mess up the electrics in the bug. Then the noise would stop and Ricky wouldn't hear buzzing anymore.

"I'll dump the bug," Jimmy said. "See you back in class."

Jimmy dashed across the playground. Lots

of kids wanted to see what he was holding, but he wouldn't let them. If other people held the bug, their ears might start buzzing too.

"Is it over?" Ricky asked. "Will my ears be normal again?"

"Not yet. The bug will be gone by Friday with the bin. The noise should be quieter when the bug gets buried by leftovers. It'll take a few days."

"So everything's finished?"

"No," I replied. "We must find out who bugged our school."

Knowing criminals had bugged our school was bad. Finding the bug in the nursery was even worse. It meant the bad guys were using little nursery kids to hide their naughtiness. One of the nursery kids could even be working with the bad guys...

"Ricky, meet me here at afternoon

breaktime."

"Why?"

"One of the nursery kids might've bugged the school."

"No way! We wouldn't do that. It's naughty. We're all really good!"

"One of you might be *pretending* to be really good. When no one else is around, they might be really bad instead."

"How can we find out who the bad nursery guy is?"

"I need to ask the nursery kids some questions, but I can't do it from this side of the gate."

"Why not?"

"Because the bad nursery guy will see me standing here asking questions. If the bad guys figure out what we're doing, they'll hide another bug somewhere. We'd have to check the whole school again!"

"So you're going to…"

Ricky gasped, his mouth wide open.

"Yes," I whispered, "I'm going into the nursery area…without permission!"

Ricky checked over his shoulder and moved closer to the nursery gate. He pulled me down so he could whisper in my ear.

"The last kid who came in here without permission got *detention*!"

I froze.

Detention? I'd never been in detention before. Only the really bad kids got detention.

Detention kids weren't allowed to go outside and have fun like everyone else. They had to stay inside at morning, lunch and afternoon breaktime.

And, worst of all, the school wrote a letter to their parents. If the student was very, very naughty, detention could last all week.

"Detention?" I asked. My whole body was shaking. "Just for going into the nursery without permission? I thought people only got told off!"

I couldn't get detention. People who got detention couldn't be Prefects. They also couldn't be police officers.

The Children's Police Force didn't want naughty police officers working for them. If I got detention, I would lose my badge. I loved being a police officer. It was the best job in the world!

But I had to solve the case. I had to find out who bugged our school. I couldn't let the bad guys win. They were naughty and needed to be told off!

"I'm going into the nursery area, but I need your help."

"I'll...I'll do it," Ricky mumbled.

"Good!"

The bell rang. Lunchtime break was over. Back to class.

"I'll be back at afternoon breaktime," I told him. "If we work together, I can get in and out of the nursery without being caught."

Ricky kept looking around nervously. He looked as scared as I felt. I didn't want to get into trouble. I didn't want him getting into trouble either, but I had to find the bad nursery guy.

All I had to do was sneak around the nursery. There were many places to hide like bushes, the playhouse and the sandpit. I could even hide under the water table.

As long as I didn't bump into the nursery teacher, Mr Benson, I'd be okay. If Ricky or Jimmy kept Mr Benson busy, I could take a good look around and be done in ten minutes or so.

If there was enough time, I'd talk to each nursery kid and find out if anyone's been acting strangely.

"Are you sure about this?" Ricky asked. "Maybe we should try something else?"

"Don't worry about it," I said. "It'll all be just fine...I hope."

I was trying to stay positive, but I had a feeling that things wouldn't go so well. Unfortunately, that bad feeling was right...

Chapter 7

The bell rang. It was afternoon breaktime. I walked as fast as I could downstairs. We weren't allowed to run inside because we might hurt ourselves.

Jimmy rushed behind me with his handcuffs and badge. We had to be ready to arrest the bad guys in the nursery. Being small and cute didn't matter. If there was a naughty nursery student, they'd be taken to detention right away.

At the nursery gate, Jimmy and I watched the nursery kids come out to play. They were very noisy for such small people. Always splashing in the water table, laughing in the sandpit or chatting by the really big toybox.

"The good old days," Jimmy said. "That's what my grandad always says."

Jimmy was right. Being at nursery was the best time I'd ever had at school. I missed those days of just playing around. No hard tests, tough projects, no tricky homework. Just fun games, cool toys and nice naps.

But I didn't come back to nursery to play around. I came to find the bad guys who bugged our school. Then I could stop Ricky's ears from buzzing.

Our plan was simple: Jimmy would keep the nursery teacher busy while I sneaked around. He was good at talking to teachers and I was good at sneaking without getting caught. With only fifteen minutes for afternoon break, we had to be very quick!

"Here comes Mr Benson," Jimmy said quietly. "When he goes back inside, go hide in the playhouse."

Mr Benson was the nursery teacher. All the girls fancied him. I think it was his big blue eyes, his shiny black hair, his warm smile, and he was great at finger painting.

"You okay, Mya?" Jimmy nudged me in the side. "Why're you staring at him like that?"

"Nothing." My cheeks felt all hot but they didn't turn pink. I'm a black person, so my skin doesn't change colour like that. "I'm fine, honest!"

Mr Benson waved at us. We waved back. Then he went back inside.

"Go!" Jimmy cried.

He opened the nursery gate so I rushed inside. I squeezed into the playhouse and shut the door behind me. Gasping for air, I waited for a minute before peeking through the curtains.

Ricky appeared outside the playhouse window. I gave him a nod, so he went inside the nursery building. A moment later, he came back out with Mr Benson. Together, they walked to the nursery gate where Jimmy was waiting.

"Hello, Mr Benson," Jimmy said. "How are you today?"

"Fine thanks, James." Mr Benson patted Jimmy on the head. "Where did Mya get to?"

"She went to the toilet."

"Well, when you've gotta go you've gotta go." Mr Benson laughed. "Richard said you had some questions to ask me about teaching. Go ahead. I'm all ears."

"I'd like to be a teacher just like you. Do you think I can do it?"

"Of course, James. All you need to do

is…"

While Mr Benson was chatting away, I sneaked out of the playhouse and ran over to the sandpit. I jumped inside and pulled sand over me until I was almost completely covered. Only my eyes were poking out. I didn't want any sand getting on them.

"That's *my* toy!" a girl cried. "Give it back!"

Mr Benson spun round and rushed across the nursery playground. He told the girls off. On his way back to Jimmy, Mr Benson looked down at the sandpit and stopped.

Our eyes fixed on each other. I gulped, my heart racing.

"So adorable," he said. "Have fun in there, little one!"

Off he went back to the nursery gate.

"Sorry, James," Mr Benson said. "There was a minor disagreement I had to sort out.

Any more questions?"

"How is being a nursery teacher different from teaching much older kids?" Jimmy asked. "Could you give me ten ways it's different?"

"Ten, eh?" Mr Benson laughed. "That is a very specific number."

"I'd like to do a scrapbook on being a nursery teacher. Our teacher told us to have ten chapters in our scrapbook. That's why I need ten differences, sir."

"Well, okay then! The first way teaching younger kids is different from teaching older children is…"

I wriggled the sand off my body and slipped past four boys getting into the sandpit. They didn't ask why I was there. Their eyes were on the buckets and spades.

The boys started arguing over who could use the biggest bucket. They were snatching the bucket from each other, and then they started shouting. Soon someone was crying. I knew any second now Mr Benson would turn around and catch me.

I ran to the large toybox and squeezed inside. Some toys got pushed out. Others stayed below me, digging into my back. It was painful but I couldn't moan about it. Mr Benson was close by, talking to the boys in the sandpit.

It took forever before Mr Benson's heavy footsteps finally went away. I peeked out and saw Jimmy waving Mr Benson back over.

"Anyway, James, where were we…Oh yes. Well, when I was sixteen years old…"

I tumbled out of the toybox and rolled into a bush. When I peeked out, Mr Benson was looking my way. He squinted like he could see something, but quickly shrugged it off.

The nursery door was close by. Just a few steps past the water table and I'd be inside. As long as Jimmy kept Mr Benson talking, I could sneak around the nursery. I'd look for more bugs and ask the nursery kids some questions. They might have seen who buried the bug in the sandpit.

"What about your exams?" Jimmy asked. "Were they really hard? Could you tell me about every single exam you took?"

"I don't remember them all, but I do remember a particularly hard exam we sat when I was twenty…"

Mr Benson was chatting away again. It was time for me to get moving!

When the nursery door opened, I ran for it. It was hard dodging the nursery kids running around. Then I had to jump over some toy cars and trains. There were crayons lying on the ground, so I was careful to step around those.

"Almost there," I told myself. "Just get past the water table and hide inside!"

There were two boys playing in the water table. They scooped up water in cups and poured it on the ground. Now there were small puddles on the hard floor tiles.

When I ran past the water table, my foot slipped on the wet tiles. I slid across the ground, trying to grab onto something, but there was nothing there. All I could do was close my eyes and hope I didn't get hurt.

Luckily, I wasn't hurt. I slid past the door and managed to grab the handle. I held on while my feet slid to a stop on the doormat. Huffing away, I just stood there in shock.

The nursery kids gathered around me and giggled. They found me slipping about very funny. I wasn't laughing, though. My heart was beating faster than ever.

All the nursery kids' laughter got Mr Benson's attention. He stormed over and stood by me, hands on hips.

"Mya, what on earth are you doing in here?"

I didn't know what to say. All I could do was let go of the door handle and fall to the floor.

"I want some answers, young lady." Mr Benson started tapping his foot. "James, do you have anything to do with this?"

We all turned to look at the nursery gate. There was no one there.

"I'll track him down later," Mr Benson said. "Mya, I want an explanation from you right now. The nursery is off limits to older children without a teacher's permission. Do you have written or verbal permission?"

"I...I...I...No."

"I am very sorry to do this, but you have

left me with no alternative."

Mr Benson went into the nursery and picked up the phone by the door. He pushed a button and turned away from me.

"Hello," he said. "Yes, thank you Mandy."

Mandy was the receptionist. She was so sweet to everyone. Mr Benson was usually nice too, but right now his white face was turning dark red. I'd never seen him so angry before. It almost made me cry.

"Mandy, I need to speak with Mr Badal, please."

Mr Badal was our headteacher. He was the meanest headteacher in the whole universe. It didn't matter what I said or did now. When Mr Badal came, I would be in SERIOUS trouble.

"Oh, really?" Mr Benson said. "You can send him instead, I suppose."

Send who? I wondered.

"Is he stricter than Mr Badal?" Mr Benson cried. "Well, she does need a good talking to. Since he's on his way already, he'll have to do."

My teeth were chattering and my body was trembling. Being told off by Mr Badal was bad enough, but it sounded like Mandy had sent someone even meaner. I couldn't think of who it could possibly be.

Knock knock.

"I didn't want to do this, Mya," Mr Benson said. "You were such a good student. Always so well-behaved."

I couldn't even speak. Tears were in my eyes. All I could do was imagine losing my police badge.

I'm in big trouble now, I thought. Anyone who goes past the nursery gate without permission gets detention!

Detention? Me? Me in detention?

I started crying.

Tears were streaming down my cheeks. Some of the nursery kids gave me a big hug. That made me feel a little better.

"I'm *so* disappointed in you," Mr Benson said. "It's like my mother always says: sometimes good people do bad things."

With a sorry look, he shook his head before reaching for the classroom door handle. Turning it slowly, he pulled the door open and stepped to the side.

"Oh," he cried, his eyes widening, "it's *you…*"

Chapter 8

Jamar marched past Mr Benson and walked straight over to me. He glared at me, his light brown face turning dark red.

"What're you doing in the nursery?" Jamar barked. "Did you have permission to be here?"

"Um…"

"Stand up and speak up," Jamar ordered. "I asked if you have permission to be in the nursery or not!"

I stood up and hung my head in shame. I wasn't feeling sad now Jamar was there, but I had to pretend to be sad so Mr Benson didn't realise we knew each other.

"I don't have permission, Prefect Sir."

"This is unacceptable behaviour." Jamar put his hands behind his back and turned away. "What's your name?"

"Mya Dove."

"Miss Dove, you are very lucky Mr Badal was busy today. But if you think I'm going to be easy on you, think again, young lady!"

"Don't be too hard on her," Mr Benson said, coming over to me. He patted me on the head, a guilty look on his face. "She's upset enough as it is."

"Mr Benson, I believe she needs to be taught an important lesson about coming to the nursery without permission."

Jamar turned back to me and stepped closer, glaring down his nose at me.

"Since you wanted to be in the nursery so

badly, you can stay here for the rest of breaktime…and clean up this mess!"

I was happy to see him, but I wasn't happy about putting away paint pots, toys, coats, lunchboxes and other things the nursery kids left lying around.

"Mr Benson, I'll keep a very, very close eye on her." Jamar took me by the hand and squeezed gently. I squeezed back. "Sir, you go outside and relax on the bench. It's a nice sunny day."

"But—"

"Unless you want to call Mr Badal and ask him if this punishment is okay." Jamar went over and picked up the phone. "Mr Badal is very busy today, so he'll be *furious* that you disturbed him. He's in a very important meeting right now. That's why Mandy sent me instead."

Mr Benson's face turned pale when he

heard Mr Badal's name. Our headteacher was so mean he even told teachers off. Sometimes it felt like Mr Badal was the dad and the teachers were his children.

"I don't want to disturb Mr Badal," Mr Benson said, his face sweaty. "I'll just wait outside for the rest of breaktime."

Mr Benson hurried out. On the way, he glanced at the phone in Jamar's hand and shuddered. He looked scared just *thinking* of calling Mr Badal.

When Mr Benson shut the door and walked away, Jamar rushed over to the cleaning cupboard. He took a key from his pocket and unlocked the doors.

Inside were two buckets, two mops and two brooms. Jamar reached behind the buckets and pulled out a small plastic bag. He unwrapped it, revealing handcuffs, a magnifying glass and a metal detector.

"Always be prepared," he said.

I quickly told him we'd found a bug outside in the sandpit. His eyes widened in surprise.

"No wonder I didn't find anything in the main building," he said. "I can't believe a nursery kid could do something so naughty. They're so little. I think a big kid must've put them up to this."

"We'll figure it out later," I said. "We don't have time right now!"

"You're right. Let's find Ricky. He can help us check the room before break ends."

Jamar and I found Ricky on the computer, listening to nursery rhymes. There was a colourful picture of stars dancing on the screen, but Ricky wasn't watching them. His eyes were closed while he rocked to the music.

"Ricky, we need help again!" I said.

Ricky kept dancing and started singing along. I was glad to see him having a good time, but we didn't have time to waste. Breaktime would be over soon.

"I'll clean up and check everything with the metal detector," Jamar said. "It has a much bigger detector range than yours, so scanning everything is really quick."

"But what about him?" My eyes shifted outside to Mr Benson, who was chatting by the toybox. "What if he comes back?"

"Just grab something and pretend you were tidying up too."

Jamar turned on his metal detector and started scanning the arts and crafts cupboard. I turned back to Ricky, who was bobbing his head to the nursery rhymes.

I unplugged the headphones and loud music blasted from the speakers. Ricky scrambled to turn it off while I hid the headphones in the fluffy toy pile.

"The headphones could be bugged," I said.

"Are the nursery rhymes bugged too?" he cried. His eyes widened in fear. "Wait a minute...*Twinkle Twinkle Little Star*? The stars are in space and so are...aliens! Argh! I knew aliens bugged me!"

He ducked under the desk and covered his ears. He quickly uncovered them.

"It's louder!" he cried. "The buzzing!"

I grabbed a teddy bear and gave it to him. He hugged it tightly and cried.

"Feel better?" I asked.

He shook his head. I wiped his tears with my sleeve and gave him a big hug.

"Ricky, maybe the bug is sending the noise to your ears through the computer. Did the noise get louder when you heard the music?"

"Yeah, when I put the volume up."

I pulled out the headphones from the toy pile and put them on. I couldn't hear anything. I plugged them in. Nothing. I turned on the music. No buzzing. I turned up the volume. No buzzing.

Ricky started turning the volume up higher and higher. It got so loud that it hurt my ears. I pulled off the headphones and rubbed my sore ears.

"Too loud!" I snapped.

"Did you hear the buzzing?" he asked.

"No. The music was *way* too loud! Careful. It could hurt your ears!"

"It's louder now," Ricky said. "I didn't hear it when I had the music on really loud."

"Mya's right," Jamar said as he walked past. "Very loud noises can damage your ears. Keep it down, all right?"

"But I *always* listen to loud noises. My whole family does. Our ears all work just fine.

Well, mine used to until..." Ricky stuck his fingers in both ears and started crying. "It's so loud now! I hate it!"

I wondered if the loud noises were hurting his ears, but how? I'd listened to loud music before and my ears weren't buzzing.

"Mya, did the music make your ears buzz?" Ricky covered his ears and closed his eyes. "It's still there. It's always there."

"Always?" I asked. "Even at home?"

He nodded.

"You didn't hear it at home before. You should've told me about this!"

"It's only when my house is quiet. Maybe once a week. Twice a week when my brothers go out with their friends."

This wasn't good news. Burying the bug in the food bin hadn't worked. I thought the noise would get quieter. Instead, it was louder. Now he could hear it at home too.

"They bugged my house, right?" Ricky cried. "This is really bad."

"How did they know where you live?"

"I know…" Ricky leaned in closer. "It was the aliens. They can see everything from space, so they know where I live."

"I don't think aliens want to bug us."

Ricky looked like he'd cry. I felt guilty.

"Maybe you're right about the aliens," I said quickly, "but first let's see if any *people* bugged you. If no one did it, we'll check out the aliens."

The bell rang.

"Time to go," Jamar said, tugging my arm. "Ricky, try not to worry, okay? We'll stop that buzzing noise."

Jamar and I said goodbye to Mr Benson and headed back to our playground. Everyone was lining up outside.

"Mya, don't get too close, okay?"

I kept a gap between us, just in case his friends were watching. We didn't want them asking about our investigation. If everyone heard about it, the bad guys would know we were coming for them. Then they might run away to a different school!

"Mya, listen closely." Jamar's voice was so quiet I could barely hear him. "Ricky's noisy ears are a bad sign."

"I know," I said. "Dumping the bug didn't work."

"The bug must be very loud if he can hear it at home. A powerful bug like that means the bad guys must be really, really bad."

"You mean the really, REALLY bad guys?"

"Yep," he said. "The detention kids."

I'd never been a detention kid. I didn't know any either. A good police officer doesn't hang around with bad guys.

Jamar stopped close to the Year Six line.

His friends came over, giving me mean looks. Year Six was always mean at our school. Everyone was used to it.

"Mya Dove, listen very carefully," Jamar said loudly. "As Head Prefect, I'm ordering you to be in detention tomorrow morning at breaktime!"

Everyone turned and stared at me. There were many shocked faces. Except Angel's. She smiled, twirling her blonde curls around her finger.

"Miss Goody Two Shoes," Angel spat. "I knew she was trouble!"

Her friends laughed at me. I didn't care about them, but I didn't want other people to think I was a naughty girl.

"As I said earlier," Jamar continued, "Mr Badal wants you to help me keep an eye on the detention kids. Do not be late, understand?"

"Yes, Prefect Sir."

"You're not in any trouble," he said. "You're helping the school. Do a good job and I'll recommend you for a Prefect position!"

Angel frowned and rolled her eyes. Her friends copied her. Everyone else just kept staring at Jamar and me.

"She's gonna be a Prefect," someone whispered. "I wannabe one too!"

"Prefects are so cool," someone else said. "It's not fair. Why was *she* picked?"

I joined my class and followed them inside. People gossiped about me all the way back to class.

When I reached my desk, Jimmy was waiting there with a paper flower he'd folded himself.

"Sorry about before," he said. "I chickened out when you got caught!"

"It's okay, I guess."

It was definitely NOT okay. I'd needed his help and he'd just left me alone.

But it was too late now. No point in being angry. If he'd been caught too, that would've made things much worse.

"Are you really going to detention?" he asked.

"Yep," I said. "Jamar and I will find out which detention kid is making Ricky's ears buzz. Then we can switch off the bug so his ears will be normal again."

"Detention sounds a bit scary," Libby said quietly. "Are you scared?"

"Nope," I said. "Everything will be just fine. There's nothing to worry about."

I didn't tell them that I was nervous about going to detention. I didn't want them to worry about me.

I was nervous because detention kids were

the naughtiest students at school. Mr Badal made them stay inside at breaktimes every day for a week. Some kids got more detention time than that.

"I've never been to detention before," I said. "I don't know what it's like in there."

"Just be careful, okay?" Libby said softly. She gave me a quick hug, her dark brown skin warm against mine. "If you need help, call me and Jimmy! I'll be very scared, but I'll help you, I promise."

"Me too," Jimmy said. "I know I was a scaredy-cat earlier, but it won't happen again. I promise."

It felt good knowing they had my back. With Jamar, Jimmy and Libby's help, I thought we'd easily solve the case.

Unfortunately, our trip to detention would end with some terrible news. If the news was true, the case couldn't be solved and

Ricky's ears would keep buzzing *forever*...

Chapter 9

I was nervous all morning. In class, I barely focused on schoolwork. All I could think about was the detention kids. I wondered which one was bugging poor Ricky.

When the breaktime bell rang, I sprung up and hurried out. Instead of going outside, I went down the back staircase and stopped by Mr Badal's office. The detention area was straight ahead.

A moment later, Jamar showed up.

"Are you ready?" he asked. "I'll keep Mandy busy. You ask the detention kids some questions, okay?"

The school receptionist, Mandy, was so kind and sweet to everyone. Nobody could understand why such a nice person worked with someone as mean as Mr Badal.

"Mya, are you okay?"

I nodded, trying to stop shaking. I was nervous about talking to the detention kids, but I was excited too. Soon we'd find out which bad guy was bugging poor Ricky.

"I'm counting on you," Jamar said. "You can do this!"

"I won't let you down," I said. "I promise!"

Jamar walked into the reception room and started talking to Mandy. I slipped by and headed straight for the detention area.

The detention area was boring. There was nothing to do but sit on a chair and be silent. The detention kids had to stay there all breaktime. When people were nearby, detention kids kept their heads down.

But today there was a boy who kept his head up. He stuck his tongue out at me when I walked over.

"Do you want me to call Mr Badal?" I asked. "Do you want another week in detention?"

"Whatever," the naughty boy said. "I'm not scared of you!"

The boy stuck his tongue out again. I didn't do it back to him. I was a police officer, so I had to behave myself, especially in front of my boss Jamar.

I hadn't seen this naughty boy before. He was really skinny and white with lots of red freckles all over his face. Just in case he tried to run away, I took out my handcuffs. I could chase him down if I had to.

The mean boy wasn't the only one there.

He was with two other naughty boys.

The first boy was Asian with neck-length wet hair. His hair was soaking wet from sweat. It was trickling down his face and neck.

"My mum's gonna be so mad," he cried. "Why did I flush those crayons down the toilet? Why did I listen to Cassie? She always gets me into trouble…"

Before I could ask him a question, he burst into tears. I gave him a tissue and waited until he'd calmed down.

"Hello," I said." What's your name?"

"Mason. Mason Ali."

"Mason, I need to ask you some questions. Do you want a lawyer?"

I'd seen police officers ask that question on TV shows. A lawyer was someone who helped people answer the tough questions police officers asked.

"My dad's a lawyer," Mason said quietly. "I'm definitely not calling him."

If a bad guy is scared, he might tell the truth quicker. To scare Mason, I gave him my angry face. He looked confused, not scared at all. Oh well. It was worth a try.

I decided to ask more questions before trying the angry face again.

"Mason, did you hear any buzzing around school?" I watched him closely to see what he would do. Would he look guilty? Would he try to run away? Would he cry more?

He didn't do any of that. He just shrugged and said, "Nope."

I leaned in closer until our noses were touching. His yucky, hot sweat stuck to my nose. I wanted to pull away and wipe my face on my sleeve, but I had a job to do. Getting his sweat off my nose would have to wait.

"Where is the bug?" I asked. "If you tell

the truth, I'll try and get you less time in detention."

"I didn't steal any bugs, honest!" He started crying again. "I took some crayons, okay? I don't have those colours at home. I used to, but my dog ate them. My mum got the vet to get my crayons back, but they were covered in—"

I put my hand up. I didn't want to hear about what came out of his dog's bum.

"Do you know anything about the bugs at school?"

"Which bugs?" he asked. "Spiders? Flies? Caterpillars? I like those."

The freckled boy sniggered. I gave him my angry face and he laughed.

"Mason, I'm talking about the bugs at school. They're hidden so bad guys like you can spy on good girls like me."

Mason's eyes widened in fear. He looked

around the corridor like someone might be watching.

"Do you think my dad bugged the school?" he whispered. "Maybe to see if I'm behaving like I promised I would?"

I shrugged and moved on to the next boy. Unless he was faking it, Mason didn't know what I was talking about.

The second boy was called Tony. He was a tall, black boy with fuzzy dreadlocks. He sat with his arms crossed, an angry look on his face.

"I didn't do it," he said. "Whatever bugs you asked him about."

He reached into his shirt pocket and pulled out a shiny, new Prefect badge. Mason and I gasped when we saw it.

A naughty Prefect? I'd never seen one before! Prefects were perfect. Everyone knew that. They never missed school or came late.

Never got told off. Never ran in the corridor or talked back to teachers. They always did as they were told.

"What did you do?" I asked.

"Nothing!" he snapped.

"Okay, what did the teachers say you did?"

"They said I used my badge to help naughty kids. They said I let my friends run in the corridor. They said I let my friends take extra glitter in art class. They said I let my friends sneak in five minutes late."

"Are they telling the truth?" I asked.

"…Anyway, what do you need help with?"

I gently pulled him away from the freckled mean boy, who kept his narrow eyes on us.

Tony and I sat beside Mason. From his seat, Mason kept looking up and down the corridor. He must have been looking for bugs.

Before I could speak, Tony whispered in

my ear, "What's the password?"

"The password?"

I wasn't sure which password he was talking about. Did he mean the password to my dad's email? Or the password to the burglar alarm at our house? Or did he mean the secret police password we used at school?

Tony gently tapped his foot three times.

I tapped mine twice.

He tapped his once.

"What's the password?" he asked again.

"Children's Police Force," I whispered.

Tony opened his shirt pocket so I could see inside. Tucked away beneath a soggy tissue was a police badge.

"What're you doing here?" I asked.

"I'm undercover," he whispered.

Undercover means a police officer pretends to be friends with bad guys. When the bad guys trust him, they start talking about all the naughty things they do in secret. Once the undercover police officer hears about all the naughtiness, he goes back to the police officers and tells them everything.

"What have you found out?" I asked.

"Nothing much from these two," he whispered. "Mason didn't hide the bugs at school. He's always in detention or in class studying hard. He doesn't have time to hide tiny microphones around school."

"And what about the other boy?"

"Howard," Tony said. "He knows something, but he won't tell me anything. Maybe *you* can try."

I stood up, but before I walked away, Tony grabbed my sleeve and gave me the meanest look.

"I told you already, I didn't do any of that stuff!" he snapped. "I shouldn't be here."

He winked at me.

"Oh yes you did!" I wagged my finger at him. "You're a *very* naughty boy. Stay in detention with the other naughty kids."

"I *hate* you," he spat. "Don't talk to me ever again!"

Tony crossed his arms and sat back. It looked like he really did hate me! He was a great undercover police officer. The other boys would never figure out the truth.

I took a very deep breath before heading over to Howard, the freckled boy. He was staring at his shoes until he saw me. He gave me a cheeky grin and winked.

"Hello, Mya."

"How'd you know my name?" I asked.

Maybe he heard my name over the bug? I thought. He might even know Tony is an undercover police officer!

"I guess my boy Tony didn't tell you anything," he said. "Good. You cops are too nosy!"

Phew! He didn't know Tony was a police officer, but he knew *I* was one. How did he know that? What else did he know? I had to find out, and fast. Breaktime was over in five minutes.

Howard looked like a know-it-all. I couldn't let him beat me. A good police officer knows how to stay in control, even if things aren't going as planned.

Just stay calm, I thought to myself. He wants to annoy you. Don't let him!

"Okay, so you know I'm an officer...so what?" I yawned, acting like he didn't bother me. "Tell me about the bugs."

"I didn't see anything. I didn't do anything." He sat back in his chair and placed both hands behind his head. "Gimme a chocolate bar and I might tell you something you'd like to know..."

I didn't have any chocolate to give him. My mum hadn't given me any that day. She usually didn't. I didn't mind, though. I preferred fruits for lunch. Chocolate tasted nice but grapes tasted a billion times better.

"Tell me what you know," I said. "I'll get you some chocolate tomorrow."

"I'm not talking until I've got some chocolate in my hand!"

I wanted to know what he knew, but I didn't want to reward him for sharing his secret. I didn't mind rewarding police officers like Jimmy when they helped, but I'd *never* reward a naughty boy like Howard!

"Just tell me what you know," I said. "Do the right thing."

Howard stuck out his tongue and turned his back to me. He was fiddling with his belt when I moved closer to him.

Hands on hips, I looked down my nose at

him and glared. His eyes widened for a moment.

"There's only three minutes until breaktime ends," I said. "I don't have time for your silly games!"

He yawned.

"You're going to tell me what I need to know now!"

"And why's that?" He looked me up and down, and laughed. "I'm not scared of you!"

"What about him?" My eyes motioned to Jamar, who was by the reception door. "He's a Prefect. The *Head* Prefect."

Howard gulped and sank into his chair.

"So what?" he asked quietly, his voice trembling. "I'm definitely not...not scared of...any Prefects."

"But you're scared of Mr Badal, right?"

Howard grabbed his chair and held on so tightly his knuckles turned whiter.

"That Prefect knows Mr Badal VERY well. If you don't tell me everything you know, the Head Prefect will tell Mr Badal you misbehaved in detention."

"He wouldn't do that, would he?"

"Anyone who misbehaves in detention gets four weeks' more detention…in Mr Badal's office!" I leaned in closer, glaring at him. "Do you want detention in Mr Badal's office for a month?"

Howard gasped and covered his mouth with both hands. He shook his head, his eyes moving towards Mr Badal's door.

"Then tell me what you know," I said. "And hurry up!"

"But…" He bit his lip for a moment. "You won't like what I have to say."

"I don't care," I said. "I'm a big girl. I'll be nine soon. I can take it!"

"I heard you whispering to Mason.

Someone can hear a buzzing noise, right?"

"Yep. What about it?"

"I don't know if it's a bug buzzing or not, but I do know that…"

"That what?"

"That you can't stop the noise," he said. "No one can…"

Chapter 10

Howard, a detention kid, said Ricky's ears would keep buzzing forever. Could I trust a bad boy like him? Was he telling the truth?

Then I remembered what Mr Benson, the nursery teacher, told me earlier: "Sometimes good people do bad things."

Maybe it worked the other way around too: sometimes bad people do good things. Telling the truth about the buzzing was a good thing, even though Howard was a bad boy.

"How do you know the buzzing can't be

stopped?" I asked. "Who told you that?"

"My big sister has buzzing ears too," Howard said. "She went to a big party with some older kids. There was really, REALLY loud music in the house. When she went outside, she could hear buzzing."

"She couldn't stop it?"

He nodded. "The buzzing stayed. It's been there all year."

Poor Ricky. Would the buzzing stay with him too? I wouldn't let that happen. I'd promised to make the buzzing stop, and that's exactly what I would do.

"I think some really bad guys put microphones in our school." I leaned in closer and whispered, "They could be listening to us right now."

Howard lowered his voice and asked, "Are the bad guys students or teachers?"

"My friend checked the teachers for bugs,

but didn't find any. We just need to check the students."

What I didn't understand was how the bad guys had bugged Howard's big sister. Was she a student too? I asked him.

"She's eighteen. She's at uni, not primary school."

Universities were the biggest schools in the world. All the students were older and got to live away from home. After leaving university, they had to start working.

"If your sister is at uni, how did the bad guys bug her?"

He shrugged.

"Maybe she was bugged when she studied here," I said. "Maybe the bug stayed in her ears when she left."

"You're wrong," he said with a smirk. "She didn't come to this school. She went to East James School."

A different school? But I thought the bad guys were at *our* school? Were the bugs in different schools across the country? Maybe the bad guys were bugging students around the world!

"Mya, I don't like you or anything but…" Howard took a quick look around before whispering, "Be careful, okay? I'm always naughty and mean, but even these bad guys sound scary to me."

Thinking of bad guys bugging schools around the world made me angry. I didn't like them watching or listening to us.

The bell rang.

"Thanks for your help, Mandy!" Jamar cried, waving me over. We walked down the corridor but kept away from each other and talked very quietly. I could just about hear him.

"You'll never guess what he told me," I

whispered.

"I heard everything."

How? He'd been talking to Mandy at the time. He kept her busy so she wouldn't catch me with the detention kids.

"I can talk to one person and listen to another at the same time," he said. "It's easy when you practise."

No wonder he's the best police officer at school, I thought. I want to be just like him when I grow up.

"I can't believe what he said," Jamar whispered. "A bug in a different school? How many bugs are out there?"

"And we still haven't found the other bugs in our school yet!"

"I checked all the teachers and each classroom in the main building."

"You checked the nursery too," I said. "If it's not a naughty teacher hiding bugs then it must be a naughty student, or students working together."

"We'll find out when I check everyone in school assembly. They can't hide from us then!"

We joined our classes on the way upstairs. The staircase was so packed and noisy that no one noticed Jamar and I while we talked.

"Mya, I don't think it's a student bugging us," he said. "If other schools are bugged too then the bad guys must be really smart and powerful. How else could they bug lots of schools without anyone knowing?"

"So we're looking for someone who can go to any school and bug it without being noticed?"

"Exactly," he said. "This person can go into a school and blend in with everyone else. That's why no one realises the person is hiding microphones everywhere."

My mind was buzzing with ideas. Who could go from school to school without standing out? Who had permission to go anywhere they liked at school?

"The cleaners," I said. "They can go to different schools, right?"

"Maybe, but I was thinking of school inspectors. Whenever they visit, they're allowed to go anywhere they like."

A school inspector! Of course! An inspector hadn't been to our school in a while. Sometimes they surprised us. Other times we knew they were coming.

"What if the inspector comes today?" I asked. "When we're all in assembly, the inspector could bug the whole school!"

Jamar nodded in agreement.

"Mya, I think you're right. Assembly would be a great time to bug the school. You know what this means, right?"

"We're skipping assembly…"

Nobody was allowed to skip assembly unless they were sick.

"What if we're caught?" I asked.

"We won't be." He smiled. "Trust me."

Jamar was the best police officer at school. He must've sneaked around many times without being caught.

"I've got a plan," he said. "We won't get caught, okay? Don't worry about it."

I trusted him, but I was still worried. There was a big chance that people would notice we weren't in assembly. Then we'd be in big trouble.

But we had to stop the inspector from bugging schools. School inspectors were supposed to make sure we had a good school with good teachers. They weren't supposed to hide bugs. Definitely not without asking first.

"Sometimes good people do bad things," I said. "School inspectors are good people, but bugging schools is a bad thing."

"We won't let it happen again!"

Jamar and I thought we would skip assembly, catch the school inspector and tell him off. Then we'd take him to Mr Badal so he'd be told off again.

But, as usual, things wouldn't go as planned. I thought we'd see the inspector hiding microphones in school. Instead, he was about to hide something much worse...

Chapter 11

At school, we had three different kinds of assembly. The most fun was music assembly. We sang lots of songs together. Some people got to play an instrument.

"Class, it's time for assembly," Mrs Cherry said. "We don't need any musical instruments today."

If it wasn't a music assembly, it could be a story time assembly. At story time, a teacher read us a short book. We voted for the one we wanted.

"No stories today," Mrs Cherry said,

smiling.

Uh oh…

If it wasn't a music or short story assembly, it had to be the worst assembly of them all: a Mr Badal assembly.

For the next hour, he would moan about something we'd done wrong. Maybe someone blocked the toilet again. Maybe someone was very late to school again. Maybe someone had stolen his muffins again.

"Class, there will not be any lectures by Mr Badal today." Mrs Cherry looked very happy when she said that. "Our school has been very well behaved recently. You all deserve a special reward for that."

No Mr Badal lecture? Yippee!!

"Class, I invited a speaker to school. He'll talk about something very exciting!" Mrs Cherry's eyes stopped on me. "I know a certain student will LOVE today's assembly."

She was talking about me. Not only did we have a special guest, but it was someone I'd enjoy seeing.

What a shame, I thought. I won't even be there for the speech!

Jamar and I had planned to meet outside the assembly hall. He'd be waiting near the door for me.

"Hey," I whispered to Jimmy. "I need you!"

"How can I help?"

"I won't be in assembly," I said. "If anyone asks where I am, say I'm in the toilet."

"What're you up to now?" he whispered.

"Nothing…"

Jimmy's eyes lowered to his desk.

"You're still angry because I left you in the nursery," he said. "Now you don't trust me anymore."

"It's not that, I promise," I said. "I just

don't want you getting into trouble too. I might get caught…"

"Are you sure this is a good idea?"

"Jimmy, we're gonna catch the person who bugged our school. He might hide more bugs at assembly time."

"Be careful, okay?"

"Class, let's go!" Mrs Cherry said. "In pairs, please."

I paired up with Jimmy and we went last.

On the way to assembly, my legs felt funny. Probably because my heart was pounding faster than ever. Soon sweat was trickling down my face, even though it was a cold day.

When we got downstairs, Jamar was outside the assembly hall door. He looked my way, but didn't smile or wave.

"I've got to stay out here with Jamar," I said. "If I go into assembly, Mrs Cherry won't let me come out again."

"I've got an idea," Jimmy said.

Jimmy quickly untied my shoelaces. When Mrs Cherry looked back, she saw my shoes and held her hand up.

"Mya, tie your shoelaces, sweetheart. It's dangerous to walk around with them untied."

I knelt down and tried to tie them, but my hands were shaking so much. And sweat kept trickling into my eyes, making it hard to see.

"I'll help you," Jamar said, rushing over. "Mrs Cherry, I'll bring her in when we're done."

Mrs Cherry started shaking her head until she saw his Prefect badge. Then she thanked him and took Jimmy inside.

"Mya, get to the toilets," Jamar said. "Hurry!"

"What if she comes looking for me?"

"I'll tell her you started crying or something."

"Crying?" I cried. "Is this your big plan, Jamar?"

"Sometimes you have to improvise!"

"Improvise? What does that even mean?"

"It means make things up as you go along." Then he grabbed my hand and pulled me into the boys' toilets. I covered my eyes, just in case. Luckily we were the only ones there.

"Wait here," Jamar said, before slipping out. I opened the door a crack and peered through the gap.

Mrs Cherry came out of the assembly hall and looked around. She smiled when she spotted Jamar, but then looked very confused.

"Where's Mya?" she asked.

"She went inside," he said.

"I didn't see her…"

"She's sitting with Year Six."

"Why?" she asked.

"She was really embarrassed because I helped to tie her shoelaces. Poor girl. She thought her class was laughing at her."

"Oh, poor darling," Mrs Cherry said. "I'll go and speak with her."

"Just sit down, Miss. Mr Badal is coming and he'll be mad if he sees you walking around, you know?"

"Mr Badal is coming to assembly?" Mrs Cherry frowned. "I'll go sit down. Thanks, Jamar."

"Always happy to help, Miss."

As soon as Mrs Cherry went inside, Jamar ran back to the toilets and closed the door. He pressed his ear against it and put a finger to his lips.

"I can't hear anyone," he whispered. "Let's

go!"

We sneaked out the bathroom and tiptoed down the corridor.

Jamar stopped by Year One's door. He pushed down on the handle, but the door stayed shut.

Next, we crept down to try Year Two's door. It opened, so we peeked inside.

Boom! Boom! Boom!

Heavy footsteps were trudging closer. It echoed down the quiet corridor. I froze, so Jamar pulled me into the classroom. He held the door handle so no one could come in.

The heavy footsteps stopped outside the door and someone tried to push down the handle. Jamar held it tightly, fighting to keep the handle up. The person outside sighed heavily before walking away.

Jamar quietly pulled down the handle and opened the door. His eyes widened.

"Who is it?" I whispered.

"Not Mr Badal or Mr Murphy," he said. Mr Murphy was our caretaker. "I haven't seen that man before."

"Then that means…"

"He's the school inspector. He's hiding bugs in classrooms while everyone's in assembly!"

"The school has security cameras," I said. "They'll catch him hiding the bugs!"

"Not if he stands in a "blind spot". A blind spot is somewhere the cameras can't see."

"We'll have to watch him hide the bugs," I said. "Then you can tell Mr Badal what you saw. He'll believe you. He always believes Prefects."

"Great idea," Jamar said. "Let's get moving! Keep quiet and stay back. Don't let him see you."

On tiptoes, we crept down the corridor

and looked both ways. The school inspector's heavy footsteps were stomping upstairs. He stopped for a moment.

"Only move when he's moving," Jamar said. "His loud shoes mean he won't hear our footsteps."

The inspector started moving again.

We rushed upstairs and stopped near the top step. For the first time, I got to see the naughty school inspector.

The inspector was a *huge* man with massive arms. He was so tall that he could easily touch the ceiling if he wanted to.

I couldn't see his clothes because he wore a long, black coat that reached his ankles. When I saw his heavy boots, I could see why his feet made so much noise!

The naughty school inspector reached Year Five's classroom. He knocked before walking in.

"Hello, young lady, is Mrs Tipple here?" his deep voice boomed. "Oh, *you* are Mrs Tipple?"

Mrs Tipple was a tiny woman. She was shorter than everyone in Year Five and Six. Her face was young-looking with chubby cheeks like a baby's.

"Sorry, you look so young," the school inspector said. "Well, I'm Inspector—"

The door closed. We couldn't hear them talking!

When I stepped forward to hear better, Jamar gently pulled me back.

"There's nowhere to hide over there," he whispered. "When they come out, they'll see us."

"But we can't hear them from here."

"A good police officer is always patient," he said. "Rushing messes things up. Sometimes it's better to wait."

He was right. A few seconds later, the school inspector and Mrs Tipple walked out. The inspector stopped outside our classroom and tried the door handle.

"Did Mrs Cherry lock the door?" Jamar asked.

"Yes…Maybe…I don't remember!"

I held my breath, hoping he wouldn't bug our classroom. If he did, he'd hear Jimmy and I talking about top secret cases.

Luckily, the door didn't open.

"Mrs Cherry is very particular about locking her door," Mrs Tipple said. "Most of us are."

"Good," the school inspector said. "We can't have any naughty students sneaking around when they're supposed to be in assembly."

"Definitely not," Mrs Tipple said. "Anyway, let's see if anyone is still around downstairs."

"I tried already."

"No teachers were around? None at all?"

"Every classroom was locked except one," he said. "I tried to open the door but…it just wouldn't open."

"You tried Year One, Year Two and Reception…Did you try the nursery, too?"

"Will their classroom be open?"

"No, but the play area will be. Let's go outside."

They went down the back staircase. We followed as closely as we could without being seen.

It was much easier to hide when we got outside. In the playground, Jamar and I could duck behind benches or slip into bushes.

The school inspector stopped by the nursery gate and looked around. While he spoke to Mrs Tipple, Jamar and I sneaked into some rosebushes nearby.

"This would be a great place to hide it," the school inspector said. "The playhouse. My granddaughter has one just like it."

"What if they find it?" Mrs Tipple asked. "I'd hate for the little ones to break it!"

"No worries," he said. "I know this playhouse very well. There's a gap in the chimney where the camera could fit."

Jamar and I gasped. A camera? We thought the bad guys were using microphones to hear us. Instead they had cameras to hear AND see us.

"I can't believe this," I whispered. "Mrs Tipple is working with them. But she looks so nice and sweet."

"My dad always says not to judge a book by its cover. She might look nice because she smiles all the time, but it doesn't mean she's a nice person."

"Or it's like Mr Benson said: sometimes good people do bad things."

Mrs Tipple opened the nursery gate to let the school inspector into the play area. He pulled out something really tiny from his coat pocket and hid it inside the playhouse chimney.

"It's in," he said. "Now let's test it."

He reached into his coat and pulled out a tiny computer tablet. He pressed the screen a few times and stepped closer to Mrs Tipple.

"Is there a microphone built-in?" she asked.

He held the tablet to her ear and her hazel eyes lit up.

"The quality is crisp and clear," she said. "This is a great way to keep an eye on the children."

"Speaking of children, it's about time we

went to assembly, don't you think?"

"I'd say so, yes. We don't want them sending a search party after us."

They walked back to the main doors, chatting away about the camera.

"We've got to get that camera out," Jamar said. "Wait until they're back inside."

When Mrs Tipple and the inspector went inside, we raced over to the nursery area. We slipped through the gate and closed it quietly behind us.

I kept an eye out for Mr Benson while Jamar crept over to the playhouse. On tiptoes, he reached up and felt around the chimney. His hands slipped inside, a grimace on his face.

"Need help?" I asked.

"I can't reach all the way down," he said. "Can you see a stool anywhere? Or maybe something else I can stand on?"

"The toybox!"

I helped him carry the heavy toybox over to the playhouse. We placed it near the chimney and Jamar climbed up. Now he could reach further down.

Time was ticking. If we took too long, assembly would be over. We had to hurry!

"Maybe you can lift me up there!"

"Good idea," he said, "but be careful! I don't want you to fall and hurt yourself."

I grabbed the playhouse roof and pulled myself as high as I could. Jamar pushed me onto the roof and stayed below, just in case I fell.

I slipped my arm down the chimney and felt around. I couldn't feel the bug.

Next, I pulled out my torch pen and shined light down the chimney. I couldn't see the bug.

Finally, I put my ear to the chimney. I

couldn't hear the bug either.

"I can't find it," I said. "Where did he put it?"

"Try the left-hand side," a deep voice said. "Halfway down. Under the rusty screw. You can't miss it!"

"Oh, thanks Jamar…"

"That wasn't me," Jamar said, his voice shaking.

We both looked back and found Mrs Tipple glaring at us. Her normally rosy cheeks looked dark red. Next to her was the school inspector, who stood with his arms crossed.

"We would have gotten away with it," he said, "if it wasn't for you naughty children…"

Chapter 12

"Mya! Jamar! What on earth are you doing out here?" Mrs Tipple cried. "You're supposed to be in the assembly hall."

I didn't know what to say, so I kept my mouth shut. Jamar was much better at talking to teachers than I was.

But he didn't speak either. His eyes were wide open and staring at something stuck on the school inspector's clothes. It was a name tag.

"Detective Inspector Dean Banks," the inspector said. "I forgot to introduce myself earlier."

"Earlier?" Mrs Tipple raised an eyebrow. "You never mentioned seeing them earlier…Are you sure you did?"

"Positive," he said happily, his grey moustache twitching. "The children directed me to your classroom. We started on the ground floor but got separated on the way upstairs."

"Yes," Jamar said, his hands shaking. "Mya needed the toilet. She was desperate. I didn't want to leave her behind. As Head Prefect, it's my duty to look after younger students."

"Yes, of course." Mrs Tipple nodded. "Our Prefects do such a great job."

"I can see that," Detective Banks said. "He was kind enough to check the camera for me. Otherwise some nosy children might have found it!"

"The camera is safe and sound," Jamar said. "Nobody's touched it."

Detective Banks turned to Mrs Tipple, who looked very confused. She wouldn't have believed our story if the detective hadn't backed us up. Adults usually believe other adults, not kids.

"Mrs Tipple, could you tell Mr Badal I'm on my way?"

Mrs Tipple nodded before rushing off.

"Why did you help us?" I asked. "You're a police officer. You're not supposed to do naughty things."

"Because I have a feeling you're good kids," he said. "Good kids who're following in my footsteps."

Detective Banks headed back inside, so we followed him closely.

"Following in your footsteps?" Jamar asked. "You mean...How'd you know we're officers?"

"A police badge is poking out of your jumper pocket," Detective Banks said. "Mya's badge is stuffed in her right trouser pocket."

I can't believe I'm talking to a real-life detective inspector, I thought. This is so cool!

Jamar didn't seem very impressed. His face was blank. I couldn't tell what he was thinking.

"I became a police officer when I was around your age," Detective Banks said. "I understand how much fun solving cases is!"

We reached the main door and went inside. Mrs Tipple was outside assembly with a small tank of water on a trolley. Next to it was a silver briefcase.

"Are you ready to go in?" she asked.

"Not yet," I said. "We were wondering what the camera is for? Why're you bugging the nursery?"

"That's a really good question, Mya," Detective Banks said, smiling. "Come in to assembly and you'll find out…"

Chapter 13

Everyone looked shocked when Jamar and I walked in behind Detective Banks. Angel stuck out her tongue, probably because she was jealous.

"Hello," Detective Banks said, his voice booming around the hall. "My name is Detective Inspector Dean Banks. You can call me Detective Banks for short. I'm a police officer."

Usually it was hard to get everyone quiet at the same time, but today no one was whispering to each other. All eyes were on the detective.

"Today I'll show you some of the fun tools we use in the police force." Detective Banks stepped over to Jamar and me. "I'll be assisted by two helpers, Jamar and Mya."

Everyone clapped for us.

"Mrs Tipple, please wheel in the water tank."

Mrs Tipple rolled over the trolley. On top was a water tank with a silver briefcase next to it.

"Boys and girls, watch this!" the detective cried. He picked up the briefcase and slowly lowered it into the water.

"His stuff's all wet now," someone said.

"What if his phone's in there?" a girl said. "I bet it doesn't work anymore!"

But the detective didn't look bothered at all. He let go of the briefcase and slowly walked around the room. I watched his briefcase, hoping nothing important was inside.

When Detective Banks came back, he pulled out the briefcase and held it while Mrs Tipple wiped it down.

"Jamar, could you hold the case while I open it, please?"

Jamar took the briefcase and held it tightly. His eyes watched closely as Detective Banks unlocked it.

"Mya, what do you see inside?"

I could see real handcuffs, not the plastic ones I got from the pound shop. Next to them was a computer tablet and a thin, silver pen. There was also a small plastic box with a tiny screen on it, but I didn't know what it was.

I told everyone what I saw.

"Have you noticed anything about my police gadgets?" the detective asked, grinning.

I looked again. That's when I realised everything was dry! No water had gone inside the briefcase.

"My briefcase is completely airtight and waterproof," he said. "It could sink to the bottom of a swimming pool and nothing inside would get wet."

I was very jealous when I heard that. My hair always got wet when I went swimming, even though I always wore a swimming cap. If only I had a cap made of the same metal as his briefcase...

It would've also been nice to have a waterproof, airtight schoolbag just like his briefcase. When it rained, none of my schoolwork would get wet. My sandwiches and grapes would be dry too.

"My briefcase is made of top secret, super strong material," Detective Banks said. "I could run over it with a car and it wouldn't break."

People gasped. I knocked the side of the briefcase with my hand and it hurt. The metal was definitely super strong!

"And now for my next trick…Mya, please handcuff me."

I froze. I couldn't handcuff a real police officer, could I? I wasn't sure if it was against the law or not. I didn't want to get into trouble.

"It's all right, little one," Mrs Tipple said, gently pushing me to the briefcase. "Just do as he says."

I picked up the handcuffs. They felt so heavy compared to my plastic ones. Detective Banks opened them before turning away from me. When he put his hands behind his back, I handcuffed him.

The detective tried hard to wriggle the

handcuffs off, so hard that his face turned bright pink. Huffing and puffing away, his arms fell back down and he hung his head.

"How do we take them off?" I asked, feeling guilty. "Where's the key?"

"I'll be all right," he said. "Just give me the pen."

A pen? What did he want with a pen?

I picked up the skinny, silver pen and looked it over. To me it looked just like a normal pen. When I pressed the button on the tip, the pointy end popped out. I scribbled a little on my hand. It was definitely just a normal pen.

I handed the pen over to Detective Banks. He moved away and stopped with his back against the wall. He was fiddling with something, and then the tip of the pen fell to the floor.

Still wriggling away, Detective Banks

gritted his teeth. Then he huffed and puffed and pulled his arms apart.

The handcuffs dropped to the floor. So did the pen, which was now in two pieces.

"How did you do that?" Jamar asked. "Was it magic?"

"This is not just any old pen," Detective Banks said, picking it up. "This pen has a tiny handcuff key inside. It means that if the bad guys handcuff me, I can always escape as long as I have a pen in my pocket."

We all clapped and the detective smiled.

"We're not done yet," Detective Banks said. "Mya, please pass me the plastic box with the glass screen on it."

I did as he said and stepped back.

Detective Banks wiped his hand on his coat and then pressed his finger onto the glass part of the box. The box flashed white three times and stopped.

Suddenly the glass lit up. It was actually a screen, just like on computers, phones and tablets. The detective handed the box to Jamar, whose eyes read the words onscreen. He laughed.

"Boys and girls, this is a fingerprint scanner," the detective said. "Fingerprints are tiny marks on our fingertips. No one in the world has the same fingerprint!"

"Why does the scanner want your fingerprint?" Jamar asked.

"To see if I've been naughty," Detective Banks said. "Jamar, what does the scanner say about me?"

Jamar grinned before reading: "Name is Detective Inspector Dean Banks. Sixty years old. White. Male."

"Male?" I asked.

"Males are boys and men," Jamar said. "Females are girls and women."

"That's right," Detective Banks said, giving Jamar a pat on the head. "If I'm on the fingertip scanner that means I've been naughty. Can you tell us what I did?"

Jamar looked at the scanner. Trying not to laugh, he read, "Dean Banks didn't clean up the kitchen when he finished baking cookies with his granddaughter. We know he was there because he left fingerprints on the wooden spoon and mixing bowl."

Everyone laughed at Detective Banks, who put his hands up and grinned.

"You got me," he said. "It looks like I was a very naughty grandad...but just because my fingerprints were there doesn't mean *I* was the naughty one. How could we prove that I didn't leave the messy kitchen?"

"Ask your granddaughter," Jamar said.

"Good idea, but if she's naughty too then she might tell fibs for me. What else could I do?"

"Set a trap," I suggested. "I'd leave cookie dough in the kitchen and hide under the table. Then I'd see if you bake it or not. If you left a mess again, I'd jump out and put handcuffs on you."

"That's a great idea too!" Detective Banks said, smiling at me. "Any other ideas?"

Mrs Tipple put her hand up.

"Detective," she said, "what about a camera in the kitchen? Then we could see if you made the mess or not."

"That's a great suggestion," the detective said. "A tiny camera hidden in the kitchen would work."

Detective Banks pulled out the large tablet from the briefcase and showed it to everyone. Onscreen was a bright red thing that was the same colour as the playhouse roof.

"This is live footage from a camera," the

detective said. "The camera is smaller than my pinky fingertip. It's hard for bad guys to spot."

"Where is the camera?" Angel asked.

"I hid it somewhere close by. Can anyone guess where it is?"

Nobody put their hand up. I didn't say anything because I didn't want to spoil the surprise.

The detective pushed some buttons on the tablet. Now we could see a different camera. It showed the whole nursery play area including the sandpit and water table.

"Now can anyone guess where the cameras are hidden?"

"The nursery," everyone cried.

"Very good," Detective Banks said. "Because you have been so good and so helpful, I am inviting you to our special police education day. It'll take place in a few weeks, so make sure you don't skip school or you'll miss out!"

Everyone in assembly clapped and Detective Banks bowed, a big smile on his wrinkly face.

"I'll just tidy up my things. Then you can come up and ask me some questions." Detective Banks glanced at the big clock on the wall. "I can stay for another thirty minutes or so, all right?"

Now that assembly was over, Detective Banks took Jamar and me to the side and thanked us for helping him. We thanked him for helping us earlier. If not for him, we would've been in detention for a long, long time.

"Can you two help me tidy up?" the detective asked. "I need to speak with you in private about something very, very important."

I thought Detective Banks would tell us about a top secret case he was working on. Or maybe he'd give us real police badges to wear at school. Maybe he'd reward us with some juicy green grapes, or at least some red ones.

Instead, Detective Banks would say something very mean. It would make me wonder if we could really trust him after all…

Chapter 14

Jamar held Detective Banks's briefcase while I helped to put the pen, tablet and handcuffs away. Everyone else waited for a chance to come over and ask Detective Banks some questions.

For now, Jamar and I could talk to him alone.

"I know you youngsters want to be out there fighting crimes, but good police officers *always* follow the rules. Don't skip assembly, classes or anything school-related again, is that understood? I won't be here to help you next time."

"But we've got an important case," I said. "Our friend Ricky's ears are buzzing. He's been bugged by bad guys!"

"Bugged by bad guys?" Detective Banks looked puzzled. "I've never heard of bad guys using police bugs. Usually *we* are the ones hiding microphones and cameras. It's to catch the bad guys doing naughty things."

Did that mean bad guys weren't bugging our school? Could it be a police officer instead? Sometimes good people did bad things, right? Sometimes good police officers were bad…

"Police officers bugged us!" I cried. "They must've used a tiny camera like yours, Detective."

"Why would an officer spy on your school?"

"Maybe because we solve cases faster than

older officers," Jamar said. "I saw a TV show where it took two years to catch a bank robber!"

"We could've caught him in a week!" I said. "Two years is too long."

"Solving *real* cases is much harder than you think," Detective Banks said. "And we have hundreds of cases to solve."

"Give us some of your case files," I said. "I can pick them up when we come down to the station."

"To the station?" the detective asked. "Why're you coming to the station, Mya?"

"To ask your officers some questions," I said. "One of our students is being bugged. You said bad guys don't bug, good guys do. That means one of *your* officers bugged us."

I looked him right in the eye, even though I was shaking. I gritted my teeth to stop them from chattering.

"Mya, we are *not* bugging your friend."

"Maybe YOU aren't, but I need to know if one of your officers is." I stood up straight so I'd look taller and braver. I didn't want him to think I was nervous or anything...

"Mya, I cannot take you to the station," Detective Banks said. "I don't even work there anymore. I visit schools to invite them to our police education days. That's my job now."

"You visit schools?" My heart pounded a little faster. "Have you been to East James School?" Howard, the detention boy, said his sister went there. Her ears were buzzing just like Ricky's.

"I did go there," Detective Banks said.

"A year ago?" Howard's sister started hearing a buzzing noise last year.

"East James, you said? A year ago? Sounds about right," the detective said. "It was a school with very naughty teens. They didn't listen much."

Jamar and I looked at each other. He looked sad. That's how I felt. Sad that an officer was the bad guy we'd been looking for.

"Have you left any bugs, I mean cameras in the schools...by accident?"

"One time, yes." He tutted, shaking his head. "It was a careless mistake. Luckily I'd hidden the camera well or someone might have found it."

I couldn't believe it. It sounded like he was bugging schools!

Detective Banks had said good guys bug people, not bad guys. He was a good guy. His police education assembly was a great way to get into schools and hide bugs without anyone realising.

But why was he doing this?

"Detective Banks, I need to speak to all

your officers," I said. "I'm not saying it's you but...*someone* is bugging schools. I won't let that happen anymore."

"Well, I can't take you down to the station with me." The detective wasn't smiling anymore. "*Real* police officers are very busy people. We do not have time to play games with you. I know you love being a police officer, but...you aren't a REAL officer like me."

That hurt my feelings. A lot.

I was a REAL police officer. I had a badge, a notepad to take notes, walkie talkies and I was allowed to use Dad's laptop for research.

Most importantly, I was a real police officer because I cared about helping people. I cared about my school and everyone in it.

Well, everyone except Angel and her mean friends...

"Detective Banks," I said in my angry

voice, "give me your bugging files. One of your officers is bugging schools. Let me see your computers and I'll find out who it is."

"No," his voice boomed. "This discussion is over. Thank you for your assistance earlier. Goodbye."

Before I could speak, Detective Banks walked over to the other kids and started answering questions. Soon a crowd had gathered around him. Even if I'd wanted to, I couldn't get close enough to ask any more questions.

"Mya," Jamar said, pulling me to the side, "you were a bit full on!"

"He's hiding something. I can feel it..."

"Who cares if he is? Their case files are private, just like ours. People hate sharing private, top secret stuff. That's not suspicious, that's normal."

"The police must be bugging us," I said.

"They can easily get around schools. They have police bugs and know where to hide them. They get away with it because we can't call the police on the police."

"Yes, we can." He crossed his arms and huffed. "I don't think they did it."

"Do you have any other suspects?" I asked.

"The school cleaners," he said. "They get around schools without being noticed. They could pretend to be cleaning while they're hiding bugs."

"But they don't have police bugs!"

"The caretaker could hide stuff when he goes around fixing things."

"But why would he? He could just use the school's security cameras if he wanted to spy on us."

Mr Badal had security cameras installed all over school. He said it was to keep us safe. He added more cameras when his milkshake went missing at lunchtime.

We never found out who took it…

"Jamar, no teacher, caretaker or cleaner is hiding cameras at school. They could just check the security cameras instead."

Jamar's face was sweaty and his hands were shaking. He looked over his shoulder at Detective Banks, who was laughing with some students.

"Mya, we can't make the police angry," he said quietly. "What if they put us in jail? I can't go to jail! I want to go to secondary school next year, not jail. It'll look really bad on my school record if I go to jail."

I couldn't believe what he was saying! Was he going to give up on the case? What about Ricky? His ears were still buzzing. We couldn't just let them buzz forever.

"Mya, maybe Howard was right. Maybe Ricky's ears won't ever stop buzzing."

"What're you saying?"

"You know what I'm saying," he said. "It sucks but…maybe we *can't* help him. Maybe this is a case we just can't solve."

Suddenly Jamar's eyes widened. A guilty look appeared on his face and he turned away.

When I looked back, Ricky was standing behind me. He buried his face in his hands and cried.

"You can't save my ears?" Ricky cried. "But you promised!"

"I won't give up," I said.

I gave him the biggest hug I could.

"What about you, Jamar?" Ricky asked.

"I'm really sorry but…you might not be bugged at all. I think your ears just *changed*. I don't know why."

"Will I hear buzzing forever?" Ricky asked. "But Mya, you promised to help me!"

I looked at Jamar, who shook his head sadly. He wanted to give up on the case.

But then I looked at Ricky's sad face. His puffy, pink eyes. His chubby cheeks. The yucky snot bubble in his round nose.

I couldn't give up now. It was my job to solve cases. All cases, not just the easy ones.

"Ricky, I'm going to find the police bug that's making your ears buzz. Then I'm gonna turn it off."

I took his tiny hands and squeezed tightly. He smiled a little.

"I'm going to the police station to find the officer who is bugging schoolkids. When I find that naughty officer, I'm going to tell him off and write to his parents!"

"Mya, please don't go to the station," Jamar said. "If you go there, I won't go with you. If I get in trouble, I'll lose my police and Prefect badges."

I turned to Jamar and gave him a warm smile. I couldn't be angry at him. I understood that he was scared.

I was scared too.

"Jamar, you've done so much for me. You checked the whole school for bugs. You saved me from serious trouble in the nursery. You got me into detention." I reached up and patted him on the shoulder. "Thank you."

Jamar's friends were close by. They were giving me mean looks. I stepped away from Jamar and took Ricky's hand. Together we walked away.

"Wait," Jamar cried, rushing after us. "I'm sorry about my friends."

"Quiet," I whispered. "They'll hear you! You can't be friends with younger kids, remember? Year Six will laugh at you."

"I don't care!"

Jamar stormed over to his friends and led

them back to Ricky and me. They looked just as confused as I felt.

"Guys, this is my great friend Mya, and my new friend Ricky. You are NOT going to be mean to them or any of the younger kids anymore."

"But YOU were mean too!" one of his friends said.

"That's true, and as Head Prefect I should've known better."

Jamar turned to Ricky and me.

"I won't be mean to younger students anymore," he said. "As Year Six, it's our job to look out for you guys."

Jamar turned to his friends.

"I know being in Year Six is hard," he said. "More classwork. Extra homework. Tough exams. And next year we might be at different secondary schools. We'll have to make friends all over again."

His friends didn't look mean anymore. Now they looked really nervous.

"It's not their fault we're working so hard," Jamar said. "Year Six is tough, but that doesn't mean we should take it out on other people."

Jamar turned back to Ricky and me.

"I'm here for you guys," he said. "Ricky, I'll do whatever I can at school and at home to find out why your ears are buzzing."

"So you're coming to the police station with me?" I asked.

"No way!" Jamar shook his head. "Detective Banks sort of scares me...Tell me how it went, okay?"

Jamar patted us on the backs before walking off with his friends. They kept their heads down and didn't speak.

"Now we can't solve the case," Ricky said. "We need Jamar!"

"No, we don't," I said. "I've solved loads of cases by myself. He's the best police officer at school, but I'm second best. I started this case without him. I can finish it without him."

Jamar, the top police officer at school, was too scared of the adult police. I wasn't scared. I was braver than him and all the other officers at school.

If I solved the case, everyone would be so impressed, especially the Children's Police Force. They might promote me! When my mum got a promotion, she got paid more money. If I got a promotion, I'd be paid more grapes!

"Mya, are you okay?" Ricky asked.

"Yes, and soon you'll be okay too."

I gave him a big hug and wiped away his tears.

"Tomorrow, I'm going to the police

station to ask some questions."

"You can't go by yourself," he said. "Who will take you?"

"Someone who's old enough to go out by himself."

"You mean Jamar?" he said. "But he doesn't want to help us anymore."

"I'm not talking about him," I said. "I'm talking about my brother."

I didn't like my big brother Will, but I needed his help. He wouldn't help me for free, though. He always wanted something in return...

Chapter 15

The plan was simple: ask my big brother Will to take me to the police station. He'd want something in return, though. I'd give him what he wanted so he'd help me.

If my plan was so simple, why was I nervous about talking to him? Because he was a teenager. Dad said teenagers were hard to live with. They're your best friend one minute and your enemy the next.

When we got home from school, Dad went into the garage to work on his car. Mum had left early for work at the hospital. She took care of the babies there.

Now it was just Will and me in the house. Good. If we argued, Dad wouldn't hear us from the garage. That meant we wouldn't be told off.

After getting changed, I left my bedroom and went to Will's. I stopped outside his door and took a deep breath before knocking.

Knock knock.

Will didn't open his door. Usually he couldn't hear anyone knocking because his music was too loud. Sometimes he played the music so loud my bedroom trembled.

"Will!" I shouted. "Open up!"

"What's the password?"

"I don't know," I said.

"Wrong answer," he snapped. "Go away!"

I tried opening the door, but it stayed shut. He'd locked it.

"I said GO AWAY!"

"I need your help," I said.

"I helped you before and you didn't pay me. I'm not helping you again, got it?"

It was true, but the only reason I didn't pay him was because I hadn't been paid myself!

"I've got pocket money," I said. "Five whole pounds saved up. Do you want it?"

"I don't want your money," he said. "I've got fifty pounds in my pocket right now."

If he didn't want money, I needed to try something else.

"I just wanted to say that you're the best big brother in the world," I said. "I love you so much."

"Whatever! Sucking up to me isn't gonna work either."

Okay, that hadn't gone well. I had to try something else, but what?

"Will, I'll clean your bedroom for a week

if you help me out."

I hated the thought of cleaning his dirty room. He didn't vacuum unless Mum made him. He wouldn't even make his bed unless Dad told him off first.

"You're desperate, aren't you?" Will said. "If you're really desperate, you'll do whatever I say."

Uh oh…

"What do you want, Will?"

"I want your five pounds…and all your pocket money for the rest of the month."

"What? That's not fair!"

"I'm *not* done yet," he snapped. "You will clean my room for the next month."

"But it's gross in there!"

"Don't interrupt, it's rude!" He cleared his throat. "Next time I sneak in late from a party, you'd better keep it a secret. Next time there's a call from my school, you'd better put the phone down. Next time I don't eat my veg at dinner, you'd better it eat for me."

I didn't mind eating his veg. Broccoli and cauliflower were really tasty. But could I lie to our parents when he got a call from school? Could I keep quiet when he sneaked in after nine o'clock?

No, I thought. A good police officer should tell the truth. Telling fibs is wrong.

"I want your help, but I won't tell fibs to Mum and Dad," I said. "You can have my money and I'll be your cleaner, but I'm not telling lies for you. I'm a good officer, not a naughty one."

He was quiet. I pressed my ear against the door, but couldn't hear anything. I didn't want to interrupt him again, so I kept my lips tightly shut.

A minute passed. Then two. Then three.

Finally, after five long minutes, my

brother said, "Excuse me."

"What?"

"I just farted. You can come in now."

Holding my nose, I stepped into his room and hoped the window was open. I didn't sit down or anything. There wasn't anywhere to sit. The bed was covered in comic books. The chair was covered in dirty clothes. The floor was covered in video games, trainers and love letters to all his girlfriends.

"Have we got a deal?" I asked, offering my hand.

He shook it, a grin on his face.

"So, Mya, you'll be cleaning my room for the next month. And giving me all your pocket money. And eating my veg when Mum and Dad aren't looking."

I nodded, grinding my teeth from anger. I wasn't happy about cleaning his messy, smelly bedroom.

"You'll start cleaning today," he said, a smirk on his spotty face. Dad said teenagers always had massive spots. "You can start right now if you like."

"Okay," I grumbled. "Whatever you say…"

It took me two hours to clean his bedroom. Every time I thought I was finished, I found more dust bunnies, spiderwebs, empty crisps packets and homework that was due months ago.

"I'm done," I said, wiping my sweaty forehead.

"You missed a spot."

I looked around the bedroom. His bed was made, his shelves were tidy, the carpet was fluffy and bright, and his schoolwork was neatly piled up on his desk.

I couldn't see anything that needed doing. Suddenly Will pulled out his electric shaver from a drawer and shaved the sides of his head. He let the hair fall onto the floor. Before I could pick it up, he blew the hair. The hairs scattered across the carpet.

"As I said, you missed a spot."

I really needed his help tomorrow. Mum would be at work. Dad would say no. Will was the only older person who could help me.

But after he'd dropped that hair on the floor, I clenched my fists and stomped my foot. His eyes widened in shock before he laughed nervously.

"Chill out, Mya. It was just a joke!"

"This isn't funny," I snapped. "I need your help tomorrow after school. I need to go to the police station. I need someone older to take me because I can't go by myself."

"Mya, just relax!"

"No!" I cried. "I want to help my friend Ricky. He's very upset because his ears aren't working properly."

"Is he deaf?"

"No, he can hear everything…but he hears buzzing too. Anyway, I wanted your help so he can hear properly again."

"Sounds pretty bad. Why didn't you tell me this before?"

"You told me off for interrupting, that's why." I stopped to breathe. It calmed me down a little. "Can you help me or not?"

"Sure, whatever."

Will yawned and lay down on his bed. He pulled the bed covers over his body and closed his eyes.

I dropped my five pounds of pocket money on the bedside table. When I turned to leave, Will grabbed my hand and pulled me back. Before I could speak, he dumped the pocket money in my hand and lay down again.

"I thought you wanted it?" I asked.

"I changed my mind."

"Why?"

"I told you already, I don't need it. I've got ten times that stashed away."

"You're helping me for *free?*"

"Your friend needs help with his weird ear thing, right? I'll help...but I'm NOT doing it for you. I'm doing it for him, okay?"

He closed his eyes and yawned again.

"What about your bedroom?" I asked. "Do you want me to clean it every day?"

"Nah, just once a week will do." He grinned. "Mum shouted at me because it was a bit messy. She'll be happy when she sees what *I* did today."

"Yeah, what *you* did..."

With Will's help, I'd find out which police officer was bugging schools and stop it from ever happening again.

But there was still one problem: Dad.

If Dad picked me up tomorrow, he'd follow me to the station. I didn't want him there! He'd try to get involved and mess everything up. He was good at fixing cars and motorbikes. He wasn't good at solving police cases. That's why I wanted Will to pick me up instead.

But Dad always collected me from school. He only let Will do it in an emergency, like when our car broke down or Dad felt sick. We didn't have an emergency right now, so I needed another good reason why Will should pick me up.

What could that reason be? I thought. Aha! I know…

Chapter 16

It was breakfast time and we'd be leaving for school soon. I had to hurry up and ask my dad an important question. If he said no, I couldn't solve the case today...or maybe ever.

Early morning was the best time to ask for something because we were always late. I don't know why, but Dad always took too long shaving. My brother always hit the snooze button on his alarm and slept another hour! On most days, Dad and Will taking so long made me nervous. Good police officers aren't late to work. Good students aren't either.

But today being late was a *good* thing. It meant Dad wouldn't think for too long before answering my question. Usually if he thought for very long, the answer was no.

Mum was in bed because she worked at night. She was a midwife. A midwife is a nurse who takes care of babies at the hospital. That's why only Dad and Will ate breakfast with me.

Because we were very late today, Dad only made buttered toast for breakfast and poured some orange juice. Dad and Will gobbled down the bread, not leaving me very much. Usually I'd complain, but not today. I didn't want to make Dad angry before I asked him for something. I needed him to stay in a good mood.

"Daddy," I said in my sweet voice, "can Will pick me up from school today?"

Dad almost dropped his toast on the kitchen floor. Luckily he didn't or Will's cat would've eaten it and been sick again.

Will's cat is called Iam. Get it? Will Iam. William! Urgh! Horrible, I know. I would've called him Kitty. Probably because I was only three when we got him.

Anyway...

"You want William to pick you up? Why?" Dad asked, his eyes narrowing.

"Because I love him."

"Ha! Try again," Dad said. "I'm not falling for that." He nibbled on his toast, crumbs raining down on his overalls.

"Okay, Daddy, I just wanted to get your birthday present today." I rested my head on his arm. "It was supposed to be a surprise!"

"My birthday's three months away."

"But the gift's on sale *now*. Might not be later."

I looked at Will, hoping he'd help me out. Instead his eyes were glued to his mobile phone. He only looked away from it to grab more toast.

"What're you buying?" Dad asked. "I'll tell you if I want it or not. I don't want you spending all your pocket money on something I might not even like."

"That'll spoil the surprise!"

"But it's good to have a second opinion when buying gifts," Dad said.

"I already have a second opinion," I said. "Will's girlfriend told me about the present. She'll meet us at the shop."

Will raised both eyes from his mobile and actually looked at me. Usually he'd stay on his phone until Mum told him off, or Dad told him off, or his battery died.

"My girlfriend," Will said. "Yeah, she could come…I mean yeah she's coming too."

"Are you still seeing that lovely girl Hannah?" Dad asked.

"Sort of," Will replied. That meant Will had a new girlfriend. He had a new one every week!

"Well, if Hannah will be there to keep an eye on you both then fine. You can pick Mya up after school today."

Yes! Yes! Yes! I was going to the police station. I could stop the bad officer bugging schools. I could finally fix Ricky's buzzing ears.

"Kids, I'll be at the garage. I'll call from there." Dad was a mechanic. He loved fixing cars for people. "You'd better be back home by five thirty."

"Yes, Daddy!"

Dad turned to Will. "William!"

"Yeah, whatever. Five thirty."

I didn't like fibbing to my dad, honest. It's

wrong to tell lies, especially to your parents. But if Dad found out we were going to the police station, there would be *big* trouble.

Mum and Dad didn't take me to the police station anymore. They said the adult officers were too busy to speak to me.

But the adult police couldn't be "too busy" now. If they had time to bug our school then they had time to answer my questions. They were being naughty and had *me* to answer to!

When Dad left the table, Will nudged my arm. "Thanks for inviting Hannah," he whispered in my ear.

Will hadn't asked to bring Hannah with us, but I'd decided to invite her anyway. It meant he wouldn't change his mind about helping me.

Dad thought Hannah was so sweet. Mum didn't think so because she caught them kissing in the basement. She chased Hannah into the garden and down the street.

I was glad that Mum didn't catch her. I didn't want to arrest my own mum. It'd be too weird, and Dad might tell me off for doing it.

"Remember what I told you," Dad said. "Back home by five thirty or else..."

I asked, "Or else what?"

"No police badge for a week," Dad said. "And no grapes for a month!"

I gasped. Parents can be so strict sometimes! Losing my police badge was bad enough, but no grapes for a whole month? That almost made me cry.

"William, I haven't forgotten about you," Dad said. "No mobile phone for a week. No internet for a month."

Will's mouth gaped open. I don't think he ever went five minutes without his phone. He even took it into the shower in a special waterproof case. He wouldn't manage seven days without calling his girlfriends!

"Relax, you guys," Dad said, smiling. "If you return home on time, none of that will happen. Don't be late, okay?"

I hadn't expected him to give us a curfew. School finished at half past three. He wanted us home by half past five. That meant I had two hours to get to the police station, find the bad police officer, arrest him or her, turn off all the police bugs, catch the bus and get back home.

I was worried about there being lots of traffic on the roads. It was always busy before and after school. If we got stuck in traffic, I wouldn't have enough time to find the bad police officer!

I also worried about the adult police officers. Would they be helpful or unhelpful, naughty or nice, good or bad?

"I hope you know what you're doing," Will whispered. "You'd better have a good plan."

"Of course I do," I said. "I'm Detective Inspector Mya Dove, remember?"

"Yeah, whatever."

My plan was simple: walk in and talk to the police officers. Be nice and be polite. If they didn't listen, I'd show my badge. When they realised I was an inspector, they'd be very scared and do everything I said.

It'll be easy, I thought. Easy-peasy!

But I'd forgotten that things don't always go to plan. It's good to have a back-up plan, just in case.

This time I didn't have a back-up plan. That was a big mistake! It was such a big mistake that soon the whole police station would be looking for me…

Chapter 17

The school day was finally over! I had two hours to get home or Dad would be angry.

As I rushed across the playground, Jamar came over to wish me luck. Libby and Jimmy gave me a thumbs up. Even Ricky was there, waving over the nursery gate.

"You sure about this?" my brother Will asked. "If we get caught…"

"Be positive," I said. "Let's do this!"

We went straight to the High Street where the police station was. Will didn't say a word when I walked up to the front door. He was too busy looking for his new girlfriend, Serena.

"Isn't Hannah your girlfriend?" I asked.

"That was last week," he said. "I'm with Serena now."

Serena was so pretty! She walked down the street like a supermodel and stopped beside Will. He took her hand and they stared into each other's eyes.

"I'm going inside," I said.

They didn't even look at me. Will's eyes kept looking over her round face and long hair. She was so pretty that I kept looking at her too.

Serena looked so different from his other girlfriend, Hannah. Serena's afro hair was bigger and fluffier. Her face was smooth with no big spots like Hannah's. I wanted to look just like Serena when I grew up…

"I love you, Will," Serena said softly.

"I think I love you too, I guess."

Serena squealed and planted a sloppy kiss on his cheek.

Yuck! I thought. Teenagers can be so gross!

I didn't want to see anymore kissing, so I went into the police station.

When I walked through the front door, the receptionist ducked behind her desk. Probably because she felt guilty about the police bugging.

There could've been another reason. The last time we met, I told her off for eating cupcakes at her desk. Drinking water is fine, but how can you chase bad guys with ten cupcakes jiggling in your stomach?

"Hello," I said. "Is anyone hiding behind the reception desk?"

No one spoke or moved. I could see the tops of their heads sticking out from behind the counter.

I couldn't reach over the counter to speak to anyone. One, because I was too short. Two, because there was a large glass screen between us. I knocked on it, but the receptionist didn't come out.

"Hello, I am Detective Inspector Mya Dove," I said. "I demand to see the Chief Inspector!"

No one came out.

"Fine, then! I'll come back with the FBI, CIA, MI5…and my mummy."

Suddenly an officer appeared from a side room. She was dressed as a cleaner, but only because she was in disguise. If bad guys saw her, they wouldn't know she was an officer.

The other officers wore a dark blue uniform with a hat. The cleaner wore an apron and yellow rubber gloves, just like Mum used when cleaning the bathroom.

"Hello, I'm Detective Inspector Mya Dove."

I held out my hand, but she didn't shake it. Instead she pulled out a soggy tissue from her apron pocket and blew her pink nose.

The cleaner dumped her mop in the bucket, splashing dirty water on her shoes. She looked me up and down, her dark blue eyes glaring at me.

I held my head high. I would not let her scare me. She was a police officer, but so was I.

"You again," she grumbled. "I've heard all about you. What is it now, Officer Dove?"

"Do you have a name?" I asked.

"Does it matter?" She rolled her narrow eyes. "Girl, we're really busy here. We don't have time for your silly games."

I didn't have time either. We had to be back home in one and a half hours. Time was flying so fast!

"Mrs Officer Cleaner, did your police station bug my school?" I asked.

"No."

"And why did you bug my school?"

"We didn't."

"We found the police bug in my friend's hair. It has your station's phone number on it, so I know it was made here."

Obviously I was fibbing, but fibbing works sometimes. It can scare bad guys into telling the truth.

"We've got your police bug," I told the cleaner. "Just tell the truth, okay?"

"You're lying," the cleaner said. "You didn't trace nothing back here!"

"I did! I held the police bug myself!"

"Show me it, then."

Oh dear…I didn't bring the bug we found in the nursery play area.

"I didn't bring it," I said. "You wouldn't give it back if I gave it to you!"

She sniggered. "Silly girl. We didn't bug anyone. Police bugs can be as small as a spot. You'd never know it was there unless we told you."

A camera as small as a spot? I didn't know if that was true or not. The camera Detective Banks brought to school was the size of a pinky fingertip. Could they really make a camera smaller than that?

"The officer you bugged can hear the bug," I said. "It's buzzing like a bee in his ears."

She looked confused. It seemed like she didn't know what I was talking about. But I wasn't falling for that. I knew she was pretending.

"Buzzing, you say? Tell me, can *you* hear this buzzing?"

"No."

"When's he hear it?"

"All the time."

"Did ya check any electronics close by? Like TVs or fridges? They make annoying noises sometimes."

"He even heard the buzzing outside at breaktime," I said. "We don't have a TV or fridge in the playground. I'd like a TV out there, though…"

"Okay." She nodded. "Does the buzzing get a lot worse sometimes?"

"After he hears loud music. Or when he puts his ear next to something quiet, like an empty can."

"Yep. That ain't our bug," she said. "Our bugs don't buzz. They're silent."

Was she fibbing? I had no idea! I thought the buzzing came from bad guys' bugs, but maybe I'd been wrong. Ricky thought aliens caused the buzzing. I didn't believe that. If bad guys, aliens and officers didn't make Ricky's ears buzz, who else could it be?

"You wanna know what he's hearing?" She leaned in. "Nothing but buzzing silence."

"Ricky isn't hearing buzzing silence," I snapped. "That's silly!"

Everyone knows silence is silent. There's no noise. Nothing! Your ears don't hear buzzing silence.

That meant she was telling a fib to make me go away, but that wouldn't work on a smart police officer like me. I knew exactly what I was doing. I'd been working on police cases since I was four years old.

"I don't have time for any of your shenanigames," I said in my angriest voice.

"Shenanigans, sweetie. The correct word is shenanigans."

"Whatever..." I knew the right word. I was

just testing her. "You're not going anywhere, are you?"

"You mean am I leaving town? No. I'm not doing a runner. I ain't done nothing wrong."

"We'll see about that," I said, hands on hips. "I need to look around. Please move to the side."

"Of course I'll let some strange kid walk around the police station alone," the cleaner said. "You can go anywhere you like. I've got keys to every single room. Just bring them back when you're done, all right?"

She's nicer than I thought, I told myself. I was wrong about her.

"I'll bring the keys back ASAP," I said. "Just hand them over, okay?"

"I'd love to, but there's a problem…"

"What's wrong, Officer Cleaner?"

"You didn't bring your parents with you.

I'll need their permission before handing over the keys...Your parents *do* know you're here, right?"

"Of course they do..."

"Good. We can call them right now."

The cleaner pulled out a dirty mobile from her pocket and placed her thumb on the buttons.

"Gimme your dad's number," she said. "I'll confirm you have permission to be here."

I took the phone from her and started dialling Dad's number. He was going to be so mad when I called him.

I bet she doesn't remember what Dad sounds like, I thought. Why not call someone else?

I dialled Will's number and held the phone tightly against my ear. I slowly moved away from the cleaner, hoping I could whisper to Will without her hearing. Then I could tell him to pretend to be Dad.

But the cleaner kept following behind me.

"Maybe he's busy?" I said.

"Or maybe you lied to me."

She glared at me, tapping her foot. Then she glanced at her wristwatch.

"If he doesn't answer in ten seconds, you're outta here!" She looked down at her watch. "Ten…nine…eight…"

Pick up, Will! I shouted in my head. Stop holding your girlfriend's hand for two seconds and answer the phone!

"Five…four…three…"

Will answered.

The cleaner grabbed the phone and held it high so I couldn't reach it. She turned her back to me before speaking.

"Hello, Mr Dove," she said, sounding a lot friendlier. "I need to have a word with you."

I couldn't hear what he was saying.

"I'm calling to confirm that Mya has permission to be at the police station."

Now all I could do was hope that Will played along. As long as he said the right things, the cleaner would never know the truth.

If she did figure out he wasn't my dad, I'd be kicked out of the station. Then I wouldn't know who was bugging Ricky and other schoolkids.

"Mr Dove, so you're saying she has permission to be here?"

I sighed with relief.

"Thank you very much for confirming everything," the cleaner said. She didn't sound so friendly anymore. "I guess I was wrong. She *does* have permission to be here."

She slipped the phone into her apron pocket.

"See? I told you!"

"I asked to speak with Mr Dove," she said, "but I didn't mean your brother. I meant the OLDER, SENIOR Mr Dove."

How did she know? Will's voice sounded deep like Dad's sometimes. Other times it squeaked a bit, but Dad said that was normal for teenage boys.

"I know a silly teenage boy when I hear one," the cleaner said. "I have four of them at home."

She pointed at the front door. I crossed my arms and stomped my foot. I was not moving from the reception area.

"Young lady, I have the power to go on the computer and find out your parents' full names, where they live and your dad's *real* phone number."

"You're fibbing," I said, my voice trembling.

"Try me, little girl. Just you try me."

The cleaner stepped closer until she towered over me. I gulped, backing away. She edged closer to me, her angry eyes sticking out. I stepped further and further back until I found myself outside.

"Go home right now," she said. "If I see you again, there will be serious trouble. Is that clear?"

She slammed the door in my face.

The cleaner was smart, but not as smart as me. She thought I was going home to cry like a big baby. No way!

I hurried down the steps and checked the main road. There weren't too many cars yet. Good. I still had time, but not for long. If the traffic got worse, we'd have to leave early. I wanted to help Ricky but being late would make Dad angry. If he took my badge away, I couldn't solve any more cases including Ricky's.

Right now, the only thing stopping me from solving this case was the mean cleaner. While I was stuck outside, she could be hiding bugs where I wouldn't find them.

Or she could've been calling bad guys to the station. If there were more bad guys than good guys, I'd have to call for back-up. I hoped Jimmy, Libby and Jamar would show up to help.

If the cleaner wasn't hiding bugs or calling bad guys, she was probably escaping! When no one was looking, she could climb out the bathroom window and run away. Bad guys did that all the time in movies.

I won't let her escape, I thought. She won't get away with being so mean!

Kicking me out of the station showed she was a bad officer. A good police officer would've helped me.

Now I couldn't find the police bugs. They

were probably linked to a computer in the station. Turning off the computer might turn off the bugs, but how could I reach the computer? The cleaner wouldn't let me near it. She was standing at the front door, ready to tell me off again.

Good, I thought. If she's at the front door, she won't see me sneaking in the back...

Chapter 18

I ran behind the police station and stopped by the large air vents. Fresh air was going in and funky air was coming out. All I had to do was take off the cover, crawl inside until I got to a computer room and climb out when no one was looking.

Inside the computer room, I'd lock the door and turn off the lights so no one saw me. Then I'd log in to a computer by guessing the password, and email proof of the secret bugs to the Commissioner.

The Commissioner is in charge of all the

police officers in London. It's like our headteacher being in charge of all the teachers at school.

When the Commissioner heard about Ricky's buzzing ears, he'd tell the whole police station off. He might send the naughtiest officers to jail for a few hours!

Before I left the station, I'd shut down their computers. Then all the bad police bugs around the world would turn off.

Ricky would never hear the buzzing noise again. The case would be closed. The Children's Police Force would give me lots of juicy green grapes to eat as a reward.

"What could go wrong?" I said. "Like Mum said, if you fail to plan, you plan to fail."

Unfortunately, there were problems with my plan. I had to think them over before doing anything.

First, what if the vent was too cold because the air conditioning was on? If I crawled in there and got stuck, the cold air would turn me into a giant ice cube. Or an ice lolly. Or a snowman.

Another problem with my air vent plan was not knowing where the vent led to. It could lead to the computer room where they kept the police bugs.

Or the vent could lead to a smelly bathroom where someone was on the toilet. If I fell out, I might land in a yucky, dirty toilet. Gross!

Or maybe the air vent led to an underground police station, where they built enough bugs to spy on the whole world!

The biggest problem with my vent plan was the cover on the vent. It was screwed down and I didn't have a screwdriver. I tried using pencils but they broke when I pushed them into the screws. My ruler didn't work either. If I couldn't get the screws out, I couldn't get in.

Oh well, I thought, I'll have to find another way in.

Nearby were two big bins. I pushed one over to the closest window and climbed on top to see inside.

The officers hid when they saw me. Obviously because they were feeling guilty about bugging poor Ricky. One of them tried to sneak out but he left the door open by accident. Now I had a great view of the stairs.

There was an officer carrying a big brown box upstairs. He tripped over and the box fell down. Lots of small cameras tumbled out.

Those are police bugs, I thought. There might be hundreds of them!

The police officer gathered the cameras and dumped them in the box. He carried them upstairs, out of sight.

The police bugs are kept upstairs, I thought. I have to get up there!

But how? I couldn't just run up there without permission. They'd stop me and kick me out again.

I must get upstairs without anyone noticing, I thought. I could climb through the upstairs windows, but how can I get up there?

I looked around and spotted the drainpipe. It went all the way from the ground to the roof. Up there, I could climb down onto the window ledge and slip inside.

If the officers spotted me, it wouldn't matter. I would've already seen the bugs. I'd quickly slide back down, write to the Commissioner and he'd send officers to help me arrest everyone at the station.

Simple plan, or so I thought.

I jumped off the bin and landed on the drainpipe. I pulled myself higher and higher, but then I made a massive mistake: I looked up!

I imagined myself at the top, looking down at a long drop. What if I hurt myself? What if I couldn't get back down? Would the officers leave me up there forever because I knew their secret?

What about poor Ricky? He was counting on me. I couldn't let my new friend down. As an officer, it was my job to protect him, even if I had to protect him from bad police officers.

Be positive, I thought to myself. You can do it!

It was time to climb the drainpipe. Sure, it was scary, but I was doing it for Ricky.

Climbing the rope at school was hard. Climbing the smooth drainpipe was even harder. My hands held the pipe but my shoes kept slipping on it. I should've taken them off earlier, but it was too late now. I was thirty centimetres off the ground. No going back now.

I could've reached the top. It would've taken an hour or three. I could've done it. I needed more time, but I didn't have it.

Then it started to rain.

Slowly I slid back down. I tried to keep climbing, but the raindrops made the drainpipe too slippery.

Soon I couldn't hold on, so I wrapped my legs around the pipe and slid down to the ground. It only took three seconds.

"What're you doing, sweetie?" a soft voice asked.

It was Serena with Will. They both looked really confused. He looked up and down the drainpipe before shrugging.

"She's so cute," Serena said, pinching my cheeks. "I love your afro, Mya."

"Thank—"

"Whatever," Will snapped, stepping between us. "Anyway, let's bounce. Better get you home before Dad starts calling to moan."

"I can't leave yet," I said. "I must get upstairs to find some top secret stuff."

"Top secret blah blah blah," he said. "Just walk in the front."

"Tried that. Didn't work."

"Tried the windows?"

"...Yes." That was a fib. I hadn't tried the downstairs windows, but I couldn't tell him that. He'd think he was smarter than me.

"Saw you climbing the pipe." Will sniggered. "Your climbing skills are pretty bad."

"Are you helping me or picking on me?"

"Both...You tried the back door?"

I turned around and spotted the back door. It wasn't hidden, but for some reason I hadn't noticed it. How embarrassing! No wonder Will was laughing at me.

"Look, Mya, just hurry up, okay?" He walked off with his girlfriend, still laughing at me.

The back door. Why hadn't I thought of that? Duh! Every bad guy has a secret way out so they won't get caught.

Now I'd found the back door, the bad officers couldn't get away. If they tried to, they'd have to go through me.

I crept over to the door and peeked through the keyhole. I couldn't see anything or anyone, but that didn't mean the corridor was empty. I pressed my ear against the door. It was so cold and wet from the rain. I didn't hear anyone coming.

I knocked three times.

I peeked through the keyhole again, but no one was there. It was too dark to see anything.

Stomp, stomp, stomp.

Keys jingled close by, but I still couldn't see anything.

Stomp, stomp.

Suddenly a door in the corridor flew open and the cleaner appeared from the darkness. She shoved a key into the back door and turned it.

I froze to the spot.

She turned the door handle, seconds away from catching me. My heart was pounding. My feet wouldn't move. It was like I'd been glued to the ground.

"I know someone's out there," the cleaner said. "When I catch you, there's gonna be trouble..."

Chapter 19

Run away, I thought to myself. You can't get caught now. Ricky needs you!

Just before the back door opened, I ran behind the bins and hid. I held my breath, hoping the mean cleaner didn't hear me.

The back door opened and she stomped out, muttering some naughty words I'm not allowed to say.

"Blasted rain!" she moaned. "Silly kid playing pranks in this weather? Where are her bloomin' parents?"

She edged closer to my hiding place and

scratched her head. Then she walked past me, muttering more very naughty words.

I tiptoed by when she wasn't looking and slipped through the back door. Then I ran down the corridor and into the first room I found.

A moment later, she stormed past, still moaning about some silly kid. If I hadn't been on an important mission, I would've found that silly kid and told him off, but I was too busy right now.

When the corridor was quiet, I turned on the lights in the room. Around me were brooms, mops, sprays, sponges and lots of cleaning stuff Mum used at home. On the floor was a security card. It said FULL CLEARANCE on it.

Full clearance? I wondered. I think that means this card opens every door in the station.

If I had a card like that, I could go upstairs and stop the bugs. Without the card, I couldn't do my job, so I put it in my pocket. I wasn't stealing it! Just borrowing it for a little while...

I sneaked out and stopped by a door at the end of the corridor. The smell of really strong coffee was in the air. Mum always had coffee before going to work at the hospital. It gave her lots of energy!

"Put the telly up!" a man yelled. "The match is starting!"

"Place yer bets," a woman shouted. "Who's gonna win the championship this time?"

Heavy footsteps rushed away from the door. There was lots of yelling and shouting. With all that noise going on, they wouldn't hear me if I moved very, very quietly.

My heart was racing when I tiptoed into

the next room. I crawled under the desks so no one saw me.

The floor was dirty and there was gum stuck under some desks. I kept my head down so nothing got stuck in my afro hair. It tangled sometimes, so getting gum on it would be really bad and make Mum really mad.

I crawled out the room and hid under the staircase. Seconds later, an officer walked past with a brown box full of cameras. I had to follow him!

Quietly I walked behind him. If he turned around, I'd be caught, but I had to know where he was going. All those cameras were proof these police officers were bad guys. It didn't matter why they'd gone bad. They had to be told off for being naughty.

The officer went down a dark corridor and stopped outside a door. He placed the brown box beside five others and turned around.

I stayed in the shadows, holding my breath. His eyes met mine before he turned back to the door.

The officer pulled out a security card from his pocket and pressed it against a black box on the wall. The door bleeped and he poked his head into the room.

"Where's the other boxes?" he said. "I bet they're still downstairs."

He walked back to the stairs, whistling a happy tune. When his footsteps sounded far away, I tiptoed down the corridor and stopped by the door. I pressed the security card on the black box and went inside the room.

It was like the computer room at school, but really dark. There were massive computers buzzing away. The buzzing reminded me of Ricky's ears. Were these computers linked to the police bugs? If they were, it meant that turning off the computers would also turn off the bugs.

The computers were all plugged into the wall. All I had to do was pull out the plugs and get back outside.

But I didn't.

What if the police bugging was worse than I thought? Maybe there were bugs all over the world!

If I turned off these computers, it might set off an alarm. The alarm would warn bad guys all over the world so they could run away! If I couldn't catch them, the buzzing in Ricky's head would never stop.

Stomp, stomp, stomp.

Someone was coming!

"Why'd he leave the boxes out here?" It was the cleaner's angry voice! "And why's the bloomin' lights off? No wonder I can't find that darn kid!"

The lights turned on in the corridor. Her heavy feet were stomping to the door. Bleep! The door opened a crack. I ducked under a desk at the back and closed my eyes.

"I knew you were in here," the cleaner snapped. She stomped into the room and stopped by the desk I was hiding under. "Thought you could hide from me, eh?"

Is she talking to me? I thought. Uh oh…

She snatched a mobile phone off the desk and pressed some buttons.

"Hello? Yeah, I finally found my phone. It was upstairs…Well, that's why I like to leave it in my apron. When I put it down somewhere, it always goes walkabout!"

Phew! I thought she'd been talking to me earlier, I thought. She must've been talking to her phone!

I hoped she'd take her phone and go

looking for that naughty kid. When she left, I could stop those buzzing bugs!

Suddenly the cleaner banged her fist on the desk, making me jump.

"He missed the goal?" she cried. "I bet ten quid on him scoring. I'm coming down! Save me a seat!"

She ran out and slammed the door shut.

"I'd better hurry," I told myself. "She might come back!"

I wanted to stop the bug. I also wanted to find proof that Ricky was bugged. Without proof, who'd believe a kid like me? People would think I was making it all up.

"Where can I find proof?" I asked myself. "Probably on the computers…"

There were ten computers. One was still logged on. How silly! A good police officer always logs out. You never know who might see your secret case files.

I opened the computer's Search box and typed in "BUG". Ten thousand results popped up! That proved the officers were bugging lots of people. I had to take this proof with me.

I couldn't email the proof to myself because I didn't have an email address. My parents thought I was too young to have one.

They also thought I was too young for a mobile phone. I could've used the phone's camera to take pictures of any proof.

With no email address or mobile phone, I only had one option left. I had to print all the proof. Yes, all ten thousand results. Those poor people had to know why their ears were buzzing. Then we could all write to the Commissioner for help.

Luckily there was a printer across the room. It was already on and there was paper inside. I pressed Print and sat back in my comfy chair.

Now I had proof that Ricky was being bugged. If I dropped the proof out the window, Will could catch it and take it home.

I'd be caught, but I didn't care anymore. My case had been solved. Ricky would be okay. I'd get my green grapes as a reward for doing a good job.

"Well done, Mya," I said to myself. "This case was really hard but totally worth it! Ricky will be *so* happy when his ears are normal again."

After such a long day, I was pretty tired.

Soon I was yawning.

My eyes were closing.

Slowly I drifted off to sleep. It was easy because the room was so peaceful and quiet.

Too quiet.

The printer should've been making noise,

but it wasn't.

Why not?

Because the computer was printing ten thousand pages on a *different* printer. That printer was downstairs…

Chapter 20

"Who on earth printed off five hundred sheets of paper?" the cleaner yelled from downstairs. "And it's confidential information! Sent straight to the reception desk. Anyone could've seen it!"

I sat up and wiped dribble off my chin. My wristwatch said I'd been sleeping for an hour. If we weren't home soon, Dad would be angry!

But where was my bugging proof? I dashed over to the printer. Nothing printed. I turned it off and on again, but nothing came out. Why not? Maybe the computer could tell me.

I sat at the computer and decided to try printing again. I didn't have time to print ten thousand files, but maybe five or so? Something is better than nothing.

"I've already asked them!" the cleaner shouted downstairs. "If it wasn't them then who's printing all this...Wait a minute. It's that darn kid!"

Uh oh. Was *I* the kid she kept talking about?

I clicked Print. When I had a few pages, I'd throw them out the window for Will to catch.

"Check the security cameras," the cleaner snapped. "She must be around here somewhere..."

I was running out of time and the printer wasn't helping. Why wasn't it printing?

I clicked the little printer button onscreen and it showed a list of every file in the printing queue. There were 9500 files left!

But that wasn't the problem. The printer's name was Reception Printer. That's why the files were printing downstairs.

I picked the wrong printer, I thought. Silly me!

I clicked the Computer Room Printer and pressed Print again.

Nothing happened.

Then the printer's tray slid out and its green light started flashing. The printer sucked in a sheet of paper and started printing.

When the paper was halfway out, the printer froze. The flashing green light turned red. I tried to pull the paper out, but the printer wouldn't let go.

"She snuck right past me, the little

madam," the cleaner said. "Where'd she go next?"

I ran back to the computer to see what was going on. Onscreen it said: "Printer Error 237519. Contact the manufacturer for assistance."

But I didn't have time to ask for help!

"What was she doing in there?" the cleaner cried downstairs. "I hope she didn't touch my new apron!"

Oh boy! I didn't have time to print anything. It would be quicker to take the files with me.

I searched through the desk drawers for a USB to save the files on, but only found pens, pencils and notepads.

"She followed Paul upstairs...Hold on! She's in the computer room!"

I grabbed a pen and paper and started writing down names, dates and anything else about the police bugging operation. My hand was shaking so hard because the cleaner was stomping closer to the computer room.

Bleep.

The door flew open, banging the wall behind it. The cleaner pointed at me and roared, "Stop right there, young lady!"

But I didn't stop. I wrote faster.

"You heard me, darn it! Stop writing this second."

I stopped writing and started running away from her. She was blocking the way out, but I didn't care if I got out or not. All I cared about was my notes on the secret police bug files. If I didn't make it home at least they would.

There was only one way out now: the window. It was a very long drop. I was too scared to even try climbing down.

"What on earth are you up to, young

lady?" the cleaner asked. Very slowly she moved closer. "What were you writing? Let me see it!"

If she got my proof, she'd never give it back. Then I'd have nothing to prove I was telling the truth. No way was she getting my notes!

I screwed up my notes into a ball and opened the window.

Down below were Will and Serena. They were holding hands and rubbing their noses together. Will kissed her nose and she giggled.

"Will!" I yelled. "I'm up here!"

Will started stroking Serena's hair, making her giggle again.

He's ignoring me, I thought. Just throw down the paper!

I had to drop the paper where they could see it. Then Will could call Mum and Dad for help.

"Don't you dare drop that paper!" the cleaner spat. "That's littering. I've got enough mess to clean up."

It wasn't my fault she was undercover as a cleaner. It also wasn't my fault the officers here were so messy!

"I know about the police bugs," I cried, "and I'm telling *everyone!*"

"Look, kid, I don't have time for this silliness." She held out her hand to me. "Drop the paper in my hand and we can forget all about this."

I dropped the paper. Out the window.

It felt like the paper took a billion years to fall. The wind and rain pushed it back and forth. Then the paper bounced off Serena's fluffy hair and landed behind the bins.

"What was that?" Serena shrieked, touching her coily hair. "Did a bird poo in my hair?"

"Dunno," Will said.

They shrugged and started kissing.

The cleaner slammed the window shut and closed the blinds. She stood over me, glaring. I looked down at the floor, trying not to cry, but my eyes were burning. My lips were trembling. Then I had the sniffles.

I imagined being handcuffed. My photo would be online, on the news and in the newspapers. I'd be the youngest police officer to ever go to jail.

In jail, Mum couldn't tuck me in at night. Dad wouldn't be there to wake me up in the morning. Will wouldn't be around to play video games with me. Our cat couldn't snuggle with me in bed anymore. In jail, I'd be sleeping alone.

And what about Ricky? Now he'd never know the truth. His ears would buzz forever.

I could've stopped the noise, but I didn't.

I let him down.

I couldn't stop the tears anymore…

I started crying.

"Poor little pet," the cleaner said, patting my head. "What's your name, again? Officer Dove?"

"Detective Inspector Mya Dove. I work with the Children's Police Force."

I wiped my snotty nose on my sleeve, even though that's gross.

"Can I call you Mya?"

I nodded.

The cleaner knelt down beside me. She smelt like a flowery air freshener.

"Look, I'll let you off with a warning if you promise to *never* do this foolishness again."

"I promised to…" Sniff sniff. "Gotta stop buzzing…" Sniff sniff. "Ricky's ears bugged…"

She pulled out a clean tissue from her pocket and helped me blow my stuffy nose.

"Look, I told ya already, we didn't bug your friend!" She led me back to the computer. "As you can see, we do bug some criminals but only when we HAVE to. They can be very sneaky, so we've got to be sneakier..."

The cleaner sounded honest, but she could be a good liar. My dad was a good liar too. When Mum's cooking tasted bad, he told her it tasted great!

"Is your friend a criminal?" the cleaner asked. "Is he a very, very naughty boy?"

I shook my head.

"Then why would we bug him?" She pulled out another tissue and wiped away my tears. "Is he a police officer too?"

"Hopefully soon. He's still very young, you know? Just turned four."

"And how old are you?"

"Eight. Nine soon."

"You clearly have more experience than him, so why wouldn't we bug *you* instead?"

She was right. I'd learned so much solving cases. Ricky didn't even have a badge yet. The bad guys would've bugged Jimmy or me if they really wanted top secret info.

"Mya, we don't *ever* bug children. That would be unethical."

"Unethical? What's that mean?"

"It means bugging kids is immoral."

"Immoral means...?"

She sighed. "Bugging kids is *wrong*. We might bug Mums and Dads if they're really, really naughty, but not boys and girls."

"But—"

"But nothing. We didn't bug him. No one did."

I felt like crying all over again. What else

could I do? I'd wasted all week trying to stop the bug and bad guys, but I'd been wrong. Again. Just like my last two cases.

It was Thursday afternoon and I had no clue what to do next. I was running out of time before the weekend.

When other kids were enjoying the weekend, poor Ricky would be crying in his room, his ears buzzing and buzzing and buzzing.

"Officer Cleaner, are you sure—"

"I told you before," she said. "He's not hearing a bug. He's not hearing anything. There's no sound there."

She put the tissue to my nose, so I blew it again.

"What about the cameras in those boxes?" I asked. "Aren't those police bugs?"

"Just normal cameras," she said. "No clue what they're for."

"So you didn't buy them to bug us? They aren't making Ricky's ears buzz?"

"That's right," she said.

If Ricky wasn't bugged, why were his ears buzzing? What was making the sound? If it wasn't bad guys, police bugs or officers then it might be...

"Officer Cleaner, do you think aliens are making Ricky's ears buzz?"

"Kid, you'd rather believe your friend hears aliens than accept he hears buzzing silence?"

I blushed. She couldn't tell because I'm a black person. Our cheeks don't turn red.

"Officer Mya, I can help your friend. I know useful tips that helped my husband. He hears buzzing silence too."

I wasn't sure if I believed in "buzzing silence", but if aliens and bugs weren't making Ricky's ears buzz, what was?

"Mya, do you want the good news or bad news first?"

"Bad, please."

Bad news made me sad, but good news made me feel better. I'd rather be sad then happy instead of happy then sad.

"Mya, I seriously doubt the buzzing will ever go away. You can't stop it."

I didn't know what to say. She'd promised to help me. Instead, she'd made me feel a trillion times worse. If she was right, I couldn't solve this case. I might lose my badge. Worst of all, Ricky would cry. A big hug wouldn't help this time.

Nothing could.

No one could.

Not even me.

"Talk to me, kid."

"If I can't solve cases then I'm a loser," I said. "How can I be a good police officer if I can't help people?"

"Don't talk like that," she said. "Sometimes we don't get what we want. Bad things happen. That's life."

"Like when Will studied for his exam and failed. He wanted to pass, but he failed. I wanted to help Ricky, but I failed. Will said he was a failure. I guess I am too."

"First off, you only fail when you stop trying. Never stop trying. Never!"

She was right. I'd never stop trying, so I wasn't a failure.

"Mya, don't be upset, okay? I never said you couldn't help him. I just said we can't stop the noise."

"How can I help him?" I asked.

"By controlling the buzzing's volume."

"We can control it?"

She nodded. "By making the buzzing noise quieter, he might forget it's even there."

The cleaner pulled over two chairs and we sat together. She smiled and I smiled back.

"Are you ready to help your friend and solve your case?"

I grabbed a pen and paper.

"Good, now listen closely..."

Chapter 21

We were supposed to be home at half past five. It was now half past seven. Lucky for us, Officer Cleaner agreed to drive us home in the police car with another officer. We even got to turn on the siren for a few seconds!

When the car turned into our driveway, Dad came rushing out. He talked so fast that I barely understood him. He said something about being late, something about being worried, and something about the police station.

Finally, he stopped to breathe.

"Mr Dove, I told you the children were fine," Officer Cleaner said calmly. "We're late because we dropped off Serena—"

Dad's eyes narrowed.

"I thought you were meeting *Hannah*," he said. "Who's this Serena girl?"

"Hannah's friend," Will said quickly. "She came with us."

"To the police station? Mya, I told you to leave the police alone. They're busy!"

Dad gave me a very angry look.

"Mr Dove, don't be angry," Officer Cleaner said. "They saw an incident on the High Street. They did the right thing by reporting it to the police."

"Oh…" That was all Dad could say. He stood there looking guilty. "I thought they were being naughty."

"Not at all," Officer Cleaner said. "Anyway, the incident is now part of a top secret investigation. That's why I can't provide any more information."

"Of course," Dad said. "I'm just glad that no one got hurt, and that my children did the right thing."

Dad and Will headed inside the house. I followed behind them with Officer Cleaner.

"Mya, listen closely," the cleaner whispered. "What you did today was *very* naughty! Don't sneak around places without permission, understood?"

"Yes, ma'am."

"I lied for you today. I will *not* do it again, is that clear?"

"Yes, ma'am."

"And tell your brother I said that."

"Yes, ma'am."

When we got to the front door, I gave Officer Cleaner a big hug. She gave me one back.

"Officer Cleaner, what's your name? You still haven't told me!"

She tapped her nose, grinning from ear to ear.

"It's a secret," she whispered.

"But—"

Officer Cleaner waved goodbye to Dad. Will had already gone upstairs to call Serena. Or Hannah. Or both.

"Sleep well, Mya," Officer Cleaner said, ruffling my hair. She went back to the car. A moment later, they drove off down the street.

I waved goodbye before going inside. It felt so good to be back home. After such a long day, I needed a break.

Dragging my tired feet, I went into the living room and flopped down on the sofa. Dad came in and sat beside me. He turned on the TV and flipped through the channels.

"Looking forward to the weekend?" he

asked. "You deserve a treat after helping the police today."

"No, I don't," I said. "Just doing my job."

And my job wasn't done yet. Tomorrow I'd finally tell Ricky what made his ears buzz. It'd be hard for him to understand. I barely understood myself.

I also had some bad news: his ears would keep buzzing *forever*. There was no way to stop it.

"What's wrong, Mya?" Dad asked.

"Daddy, I've got bad news for my friend. When I tell him, he's going to cry."

Dad put his arm around me and rested his head on mine.

"Mya, if he cries, give him a really big hug."

"What if that doesn't work?"

"When hugs and kisses don't help, try cards and gifts. What gift would he like?"

That was a tough one. I didn't really know Ricky. We'd only been friends for a week.

What gift would he like? I wondered. What gift would a four-year-old boy like?

I asked Dad.

"It's been a while since I was a four-year-old boy," he said. "When Will was that age, he loved car sets, building blocks, dinosaurs and other very expensive toys."

"I don't have enough pocket money to buy all that."

"A gift doesn't have to be expensive," he said. "The thought behind the gift counts more than the price tag."

Dad was right. I didn't have to buy something expensive to make Ricky feel better.

"What does he like doing?" Dad asked. "Is he a police officer like you?"

"Not yet," I said. "He wants to be."

"You can get him started. Buy him something police-related. If you can't afford it, make it."

I could afford to buy Ricky something "police-related", but the shops were closed now. They didn't open before school, so I couldn't buy something in the morning.

It was too late to buy something, but it wasn't too late to *make* something.

"What police-related thing could I make?" I asked Dad. "Nothing too hard like a police hat or handcuffs."

"I've got an idea," he said. "Just follow my instructions…"

Chapter 22

I needed time to get ready before meeting Ricky, so Dad took me to school early.

I went straight to the nursery play area. Luckily Mr Benson wasn't around to tell me off again. Jamar wasn't there to save me this time.

I pulled out some headphones from my schoolbag and hid them in the bushes. I wouldn't be allowed to bring them down at lunchtime, so I had to leave them outside.

Next, I took out a fake worm – I borrowed it from Will's bedroom – and left it by the playhouse door. The worm would scare girls away, keeping the playhouse empty until I needed it.

Finally, I pulled out a sheet of paper with WET PAINT written on it. I wasn't sure if the nursery kids could read, but Mr Benson definitely could. I stuck the paper on the playhouse door so he wouldn't go inside.

A door slammed shut in the nursery. It was Mr Benson! I ran out the nursery gate and ducked behind the fence.

Heavy footsteps trudged closer and closer. I closed my eyes and hoped he hadn't seen me. If he had, I'd definitely get detention this time!

He stopped by the playhouse and sighed.

"He painted it *again*? The girls won't be happy about this…" He tutted. "At least his handwriting's improved. I can actually read it this time."

Go back inside, I thought. Please don't come this way!

Mr Benson didn't go back inside. Instead he walked closer to the fence. The latch on the nursery gate squeaked and he put one foot out. I kept perfectly still, holding my breath.

"What're you doing?" he asked. "You're NOT allowed in the nursery area!"

Did he see me? I wondered. I'd better get up and talk to him. Hopefully he won't be *too* mad…

Before I could get up, he slammed the nursery gate and walked away. I peered through the fence and saw him shaking the bushes. A scruffy, brown cat jumped out and dashed across the play area.

"Go home, silly boy!" Mr Benson cried, chasing after it. "I'm tired of cleaning up your poo. The nursery area is *not* your toilet!"

He wasn't talking to me, I thought. He was talking to the cat! Phew!

While he chased the cat around, I crawled to the bushes nearby. When the bell rang, I joined my class. No one had any idea what I'd just been up to.

That's enough for now, I thought to myself. At breaktime, I'll make Ricky's gift.

When breaktime came, Mrs Cherry let me stay in class. I told her I was making a gift and needed stuff from the arts cupboard.

"Just this once," she said. "Our little secret."

In the arts cupboard, there was so much to choose from. Different colours, fabrics, textures and materials. I chose black card, gold foil paper, a black marker, scissors, glue and a big safety pin.

That was everything I needed.

I sat at my desk and got to work. There

was lots of cutting, sticking, gluing and writing to be done. It was so much fun!

When I was finished, I wrapped the present in rainbow-coloured tissue paper.

I should've asked the Children's Police Force before giving Ricky the gift, but I didn't care. After all he'd been through, I thought he deserved it.

"Will he like his gift?" I asked myself. "I hope so..."

Hours later, it was lunchtime. Instead of going to eat, I crept outside and ran to the nursery gate. I was just in time. The nursery kids had lunch before us, so they were already outside.

Ricky was building a sandcastle in the sandpit. Every so often he'd stick a finger in his ear and frown.

When he looked up, he spotted me peeking over the nursery gate. With a big smile, he dashed over to say hello.

I reached over the gate and squeezed his hand. I wanted to open the gate and give him a hug, but I was scared that Mr Benson would come out and tell me off.

"Didn't think you were coming back," Ricky said. "I thought you'd been caught by bad guys or aliens."

"I did get caught at the police station," I said, "but it worked out in the end."

"Glad you're okay. I would've missed you if you never came back."

"I would've missed you too."

We squeezed each other's hands.

"Did you find out anything about the bugs?" he asked. "How do we stop them? How do we stop the buzzing?"

I wasn't looking forward to giving him bad news, but I had to. He needed to know what was really going on with his ears.

"I met a cleaner at the police station. She told me what's wrong with your ears."

"It's aliens from Mars, isn't it?" he said. "I knew it! I told you so!"

"Aliens? Not this time, no." I pulled him a little closer. "Ricky, I'm sorry to tell you this, but you have…"

Chapter 23

"I have what?" Ricky asked.

"The cleaner said you have something called tinnitus and that—"

"That what?" he asked, tears in his eyes. "It's bad, isn't it?"

"Do you want the good news or the bad news first?" I asked.

"Good first, please."

"The good news is that no matter what happens, I'll be here for you. When you cry, I'll hug you. When you're sad, I'll hold you. You can always talk to me, okay?"

"Thank you, Mya," he said. "Knowing you're my friend is really good news…but what's the bad news?"

"Your ears will keep buzzing *forever*."

"What's the buzzing called?"

"Tinnitus."

"Tinny? Tiny? Tin? Tin! Like what baked beans come in? Like the bug we found the other day?" He squealed like a girl. "Am I turning into the Tin Man from Oz? He was my favourite character in the movie."

"No! Tinnitus is a sound that's only in your head. The sound could be ringing like a phone, buzzing like a bee or whooshing like waves at the beach."

"Tinnitus is just in my head?" he asked, tears trickling down his chubby cheeks.

"That's why no one else can hear it. Tinnitus isn't a real sound. It's just in your head."

"Just in my head? Great, I guess. That means the noise won't wake up my dad at bedtime. Or my mum. Or my brothers. Just me. Just in my head..."

He burst into tears.

"Ricky, it's gonna be okay. Tinnitus doesn't mean something bad. Sometimes it just happens by itself. Other times you might need some vitamins. Your doctor will find out for you."

I'd brought a pack of tissues with me, just in case. I wiped his tears with one tissue and helped blow his nose with another.

"How do I stop the buzzing?" he asked. "I've got to stop it! I want normal ears like everybody else!"

"I'm sorry, Ricky, but you can't stop the buzzing. Your old, normal ears are gone. Your new ears will keep buzzing *forever*."

He cried like a baby.

"It'll be okay!" I said. "First, we'll see if you really have tinnitus. Then I'll teach you how to control it."

"Can I make it go away?"

"No but...It's hard to explain. Let me show you, okay?"

I looked over at the nursery. Mr Benson didn't seem to be around.

"Ricky, go to the toybox and take out a teddy bear. Take the bear over to the door and wait there. If Mr Benson is coming out, drop the bear. Then I'll know I need to hide, okay?"

"Okay," he said. "What should I do next?"

"Meet me at the playhouse."

Ricky did as I said. When he stood by the door, I slipped through the nursery gate.

My eyes stayed on Ricky as I tiptoed towards the bushes. The headphones were peeking out, right where I'd left them. As I edged closer to the bush, my heart beat faster and faster.

Before I reached the bushes, Ricky dropped the teddy. That meant Mr Benson was coming out!

I sprinted across the play area, huffing and puffing away. When I heard Mr Benson's voice, he sounded so close. I knew I wouldn't reach the bushes before he came out.

"Spider!" Ricky cried. "I saw one in the sandpit!"

A group of girls started screaming and ran inside. Now they were blocking the doorway. Nobody could go out or in.

"Hide," Ricky cried. "Quickly!"

I threw myself behind the playhouse just before Mr Benson came out. He put his hands up to calm everyone down, but the screams got louder.

"Mr Benson, I'll tell the spider to go

away," Ricky said. "You just keep everyone inside."

"Thank you," Mr Benson said. "You're such a helpful young man."

When Mr Benson went inside, I got the headphones from the bushes and met Ricky in the playhouse.

"You did great back there," I whispered. "Thank you for saving me!"

His pale cheeks turned bright pink.

"It wasn't nice making my friends cry, but I'll say sorry later. They can have some of my crisps."

Just in case Mr Benson came outside, I closed the curtains while Ricky got comfortable at the table.

"The buzzing is louder now," he said sadly.

"No, it only *seems* louder because it's quiet in here."

"Can I make some noise, then? I don't want to hear the buzzing anymore."

"No. It must be very quiet."

And soon it was. Mr Benson called in the other nursery kids for naptime. Before going inside, he glanced at the playhouse. Would he spot me peeking through the curtains?

His blue eyes narrowed, a confused look on his face. Then he shrugged and hurried inside.

The play area was much quieter now the other kids were inside.

"We can start now," I said. "Are you ready to control the tinnitus?"

He nodded.

I placed the headphones over his ears. He took my hand and squeezed. I squeezed back.

"It's...It's...It's silent!" he cried. "Can't hear anything but the buzzing!"

I turned his head to face me.

"It's so loud!" He took off the headphones. "I can still hear it."

"It's the tinnitus," I said. "It can't hurt you or your ears."

"It's in my head," he said. "It can't hurt me."

"That's right," I said. "There's no police bug or aliens or bad guys. Just a weird noise that can't hurt you."

"It can't hurt me, it can't hurt me, it can't hurt me..."

"Good," I said. "Now let's make the buzzing quieter."

I took a deep breath, held it, then breathed out.

"Breathe in for five seconds, hold it, then breathe out for five seconds."

He breathed in. Held it. Breathed out.

"One, two, three, four, five," I counted, breathing in. I waited a second before breathing out. "Five, four, three, two, one."

Ricky joined in, slowly releasing my hand until he let go. Over and over we just took deep breaths.

"It's quieter," he said. "I think."

"Seems like it, right?" I gave him a big hug. "I'm so proud of you. You did it! You made the buzzing quieter."

"How else can I make it quieter?"

"Stop sticking your fingers in your ears. It doesn't help. It makes you focus on the buzzing more."

"I can do that! No more fingers in my ears."

I stopped to remember what else Officer Cleaner told me yesterday.

"Your tinnitus might sound louder if you go from a noisy place to a quiet one. Don't worry about it. It's normal."

"A quiet place like this playhouse at

naptime," he said. "And quiet like the police bug I found in the sandpit. I put it to my ear and the buzzing got louder."

"Exactly!" I said. "The tinnitus *seemed* louder because it was quiet inside the can."

"Why is the tinnitus quieter at home?" he asked.

"You said your family is really, really noisy, that's why. Your family makes so much noise that you can't hear the tinnitus."

I couldn't remember what else Officer Cleaner told me, so I peeked at the notes in my pocket.

"Tinnitus also seems louder when you're scared, upset or angry. Try to calm down. Tinnitus sounds much quieter when you're calm."

He glanced down at the headphones.

"I wasn't scared, upset or angry when I listened to music. Why was the tinnitus louder then?"

"Because the music was too loud," I said. "That can hurt your ears and make the tinnitus worse. Keep the volume down, okay?"

"Okay! No more loud music!"

"Oh, if you haven't already, tell your mum and dad about the buzzing. They'll take you to the doctor to get your ears checked."

"Cool!" Ricky cried. "Doctor Edwards always lets me hear my own heartbeat. It's so loud!"

"Remember to always tell your parents when you don't feel right. They'll help you. A good police officer isn't scared to ask for help."

"But I'm not a police officer..."

He started crying again.

"What's wrong?"

"Naptime's been hard because of the

tinnitus. Bedtime too. But now I can sleep good again! Thank you, Officer Dove."

"You're welcome, Officer Miles." I patted him on the head. "Before I go, here's a present."

When I showed him the gift, he grabbed it. He tore away the rainbow-coloured tissue paper, his hands shaking with excitement.

So were mine.

When he saw the gift I'd made, he cried happy tears. His fingers slid over the gold foil paper, following the letters in his name.

"I can't believe it," Ricky cried. "Mya, it's a…it's a…"

Chapter 24

"A police badge," I said. "Your own police badge."

I unclipped the safety pin on the back and pinned the badge to his t-shirt.

"Congrats, Officer Miles!" I clapped, but not too loud. I didn't want Mr Benson to hear us. "You've done so well. You deserve it."

"I can't wait to show all my friends! It's so cool!" He stared at his first ever badge. "Did you make it?"

"Yeah…Do you like it?"

"No."

"No?"

"I don't like it," he said. "I *love* it!"

Phew! He'd scared me for a second…

"Do you feel better about the tinnitus now?" I asked.

He thought for a moment.

"Yeah, I guess."

"You forgot about the buzzing noise, didn't you?"

"Yeah." He grinned. "I did."

He was so excited about his first ever badge that he'd forgotten the buzzing.

"Not paying attention to the tinnitus will help him forget it," Officer Cleaner said yesterday. "Then the noise won't bother him so much."

Bit by bit, little by little, Ricky would get used to the buzzing silence. It'd make him sad sometimes, but soon he'd think of it less and less.

One day he'd forget the tinnitus for a few minutes. Then a few hours. Soon he wouldn't remember it for days, weeks, even months. Whenever he did remember the buzzing silence, it wouldn't upset him anymore.

"I'll never hear real silence again," Ricky said, "and I don't care."

"Why not?" I asked.

"Real silence was boring."

He was right. Who cares about real silence anyway? It's the different sounds that count! Amazing sounds like music, voices, animals, nature and so much more.

The bell rang. It was time to go. The older kids would be out to play soon.

"I'd better go before Mr Benson comes out," I said. "Will you be okay?"

"Yup," Ricky said. "The buzzing silence

can't hurt me. And it can't stop me solving cases with my brand-new police badge!"

I crept out of the playhouse and dashed over to the nursery gate. I slipped through and made sure it was locked behind me.

Instead of playing with my friends, I went to tell my boss about the buzzing silence mystery. I knew she'd be so happy that I'd solved another big case!

I went straight to the girls' bathroom and locked myself in a toilet stall. My secret boss was already there, so I didn't get a chance to see who she was. Oh well. Maybe next time...

At least she'd remembered my green grapes. I could hear the plastic bag rustling.

She stomped three times.

I stomped twice.

She stomped once.

"What's the password?" she asked.

"Children's Police Force."

"Good," she said. "Hello, officer."

"Reporting for duty." I saluted. Why did I salute? She couldn't even see me! "The case has been solved. Ricky Miles is okay."

"Who bugged him?" she asked. "FBI? CIA? Or aliens?"

What's with the aliens? I thought. I've never seen any...

"Nobody bugged Ricky," I said. "The buzzing sound is in his head. It's called tinnitus. He'll get used to it, but it'll take some time."

"Interesting...At least no bad guys are bugging us. The other officers will feel much better now."

The plastic bag rustled again, making my stomach grumble. I closed my eyes, imagining the juicy grapes in my hands.

"That's it, then," my secret boss said.

"Speak to you soon."

"Wait a minute!" I cried. "What about my grapes? Don't I get a reward?"

Would she leave me without paying AGAIN? All I wanted was ONE sweet, juicy, bouncy grape. I could almost taste it.

My stomach grumbled again.

"Detective Dove, you were told to find out who was bugging Ricky Miles. You didn't do that, so no grapes for you!"

"But no one bugged him!" I cried. "He just listened to really loud music that hurt his ears! Or maybe he needs vitamins from the doctor. Or maybe his ears just changed by themselves!"

"Rules are rules," she snapped. "You would've been paid for finding out who bugged him. The big problem is, *nobody* bugged him. No bugging means no grapes."

"Gimme a break! Just one tiny grape,

pretty please!"

"No special treatment allowed or other officers will be jealous."

"I won't tell anyone, I promise!" My fingers and toes were crossed for luck. "Just *one* grape, please!"

"Go out and play," she said. "Your friends are waiting."

"Aw, but I missed lunchtime to help Ricky! I'm hungry!"

"Detective Dove, you are dismissed!"

"But—"

"But nothing!"

She flushed.

There was no point in arguing with her. I wasn't getting those grapes. She was keeping them for herself.

"See you later," I said sadly. I left the toilet stall and went into the corridor. It was too late for lunch, so I had to go outside.

On the way out, I passed the lunch hall. The tasty food smells went up my nose, making my mouth water. I stood there for a few minutes, imagining the tasty food people had eaten for lunch.

My poor stomach feels bad enough, I thought. Smelling all this tasty food isn't helping! I'd better go out and play.

Outside, I looked for my friends in the playground. They were having a great time playing games. I didn't feel like joining in because my empty stomach hurt too much. Drinking some water didn't help, so I sat on the nearest bench and rubbed my sore belly.

Mrs Cherry came outside and sat beside me. "I needed some fresh air," she said. "It's such a lovely day!"

"Yes, Miss…"

"Is everything all right, dear?"

"Yes, Miss..."

"What's wrong, Mya?" she asked.

I was sad about not getting any green grapes. I wondered if I deserved them. I was supposed to fix Ricky's ears, but I didn't. He'd feel better someday, but I was supposed to help him *today*. Not later.

"Mya, I can tell when you're down," Mrs Cherry said. "You can talk to me."

"My friend has a problem and it'll *never* go away. I promised to fix it but...I can't. I don't think anybody can."

"In life, we can't fix everything," she said. "We don't always get what we want. Sometimes we must accept things as they are."

Mrs Cherry ruffled my hair and walked off to blow her whistle. The other kids rushed over to put away toys and balls.

When everyone lined up, I took a good look at each student. Seeing the differences between us taught me something *very* important: everyone is different and that's okay.

There were common differences we saw every day. Some people were tall, others were short, and most were in between.

Some people were skinny, some were slim, and others were fat.

Some people were old like Detective Banks, younger like Mrs Cherry, or just a kid like Ricky.

There were white people like Jimmy, biracials like Jamar, Asians like Mr Badal, and black people like me.

There were brunettes, blondes, redheads and greyheads. Some people had no hair, short hair, long hair and really long hair.

There were boys and girls, rich and poor, British, Irish and other nationalities.

Height, weight, age, race, hair, gender and

nationality. Those were very common differences between us. There were uncommon ones too, like people who couldn't see, hear, walk or talk. Their bodies weren't normal.

But who decides what "normal" is? I wondered. It's normal for deaf people not to hear. It's normal for blind people not to see. There isn't *one* way to be normal.

Everyone is normal because everyone is different. My normal is different from yours. Your normal is different from mine.

My normal body could do *amazing* things! It could jump, run, sing, dance, play, colour, draw, write, watch, listen, chat, laugh, cry happy tears, fall asleep and wake up to have fun all over again.

Some people did all that even though their bodies weren't "normal".

There were deaf people playing musical

instruments. Blind people climbing the highest mountains in the world. People in wheelchairs playing the hardest sports and winning gold medals.

If they could achieve so much with a body that wasn't "normal", so could people like Ricky whose bodies *stopped* being normal.

Just like our phones and computers, sometimes our bodies stopped working properly. They might stop working for a while. They might stop working forever. But no matter what, we could still enjoy each day.

Every day was another chance to love our family, laugh with friends, and be our own normal, whatever that may be.

What was *my* normal?

My normal was being short. My normal was black skin and coily, afro hair. My normal was having a dad who worked in the day, and a mum who worked at night. My normal was an annoying big brother who I loved a lot (Don't tell him I said that!). My normal was solving top secret cases for juicy grapes.

What's *your* normal?

Whatever it is, it's okay. Being normal means being different. Being different means being you.

Don't stop being you.

Because we all matter.

You matter.

CASE CLOSED

Dear Reader

Hello, I hope you enjoyed my book. You can email me at contact@zuniblue.com. I'd love to hear from you!

I'd really appreciate it if you left a book review saying whether you loved it, hated it, or thought it was just okay. It doesn't have to be a long review. Thank you very much!

Keep reading to get your 100 free gifts...

About the Author

Zuni Blue lives in London, England with her parents. She's been writing non-fiction and fiction since she was a kid.

She loves telling stories that show how diverse the world is. Her characters are different races, genders, heights, weights and live with various disabilities and abilities. In Zuni's books, every child is special!

Solve More Cases

Would you like to read another case file?

Mya doesn't share her cases with just anyone, but she knows she can trust you.

Keep reading for more top secret cases she's solved...

The Parents With A Sleepover Secret

Mya has to stay at her enemy Angel's house. Angel is forcing her to solve a tough case. If the case isn't solved, Mya will be kicked off the Children's Police Force!

To solve the mystery, Detective Dove must face an angry poodle, a scary garage, and the meanest girl in the universe...

The Fat Girl Who Never Eats

Ten school burgers were stolen. Everyone blames the fat girl, but no one saw her do it. Is she the burger thief or is it someone else?

To solve the mystery, Detective Dove must face her crafty dad, a strange caretaker, and the shocking secret in the school basement...

The Mean Girl Who Never Speaks

There's a new girl at school. She never speaks, never smiles and never plays with other kids. Does that mean she's mean? Maybe. Maybe not...

To solve the mystery, Detective Dove must face a suspicious teacher, the school bully, and the meanest boss in the world...

The School Pet Who Went Missing

Mya's school has a brand new pet. It's cute, cuddly and loves everyone. Unfortunately, it's gone missing! Did it run away? Or was it stolen?

To solve the mystery, Detective Dove must face her bossy headmaster, a mean prefect, and a sneaky teacher with a dark secret...

Dedications

This book is dedicated to anyone with hearing problems, particularly tinnitus. I've learned to live with it. You can too.

Thank you to my family and friends. I appreciate all the love and support you have given me. I couldn't have done this without you.

An extra special thank you to every reader who's emailed me. I love hearing from you!

100 Free Gifts For You

There are 100 FREE printables waiting for you!

Certificates, bookmarks, wallpapers and more! You can choose your favourite colour: red, yellow, pink, green, orange, purple or blue.

You don't need money or an email address. Check out www.zuniblue.com to print your free gifts today.

Made in the USA
Columbia, SC
14 May 2020